Grim Hill
The
Forgotten
Secret

Published by Lobster Press™
1620 Sherbrooke Street West, Suites C & D
Montréal, Québec   H3H 1C9
Tel. (514) 904-1100 • Fax (514) 904-1101 • www.lobsterpress.com

Publisher: Alison Fripp
Editor: Meghan Nolan
Editorial Assistants: Susanna Rothschild & Erin Simnitt
Cover Illustration: John Shroades
Graphic Design & Production: Tammy Desnoyers

We acknowledge the financial support of the Government of Canada
through the Book Publishing Industry Development Program (BPIDP)
for our publishing activities.

We acknowledge the support of the Canada
Council for the Arts for our publishing program.

The Canada Council | Le Conseil des Arts
for the Arts | du Canada

Library and Archives Canada Cataloguing in Publication

DeMeulemeester, Linda, 1956-
    Grim Hill : the forgotten secret / Linda DeMeulemeester.

(Grim Hill ; #3)
ISBN 978-1-897550-13-7

    I. Title. II. Title: Forgotten secret. III. Series: DeMeulemeester,
Linda, 1956- . Grim Hill ; #3

PS8607.E58G745 2009   jC813'.6   C2008-905585-3

Printed and bound in Canada.

Praise for the "Grim Hill" series:

"... solid tween appeal ..." – *The Globe and Mail*

"... a pre-Steven King novel for tween readers."
– *BellaOnline.com*

"... a protagonist who is self-centred enough to be
interesting, a precocious kid sister who deserves her own
book and a plot that bubbles along at a magical pace ...
creepy enough to cast a spell over anyone who reads it!"
– *Resource Links*

"DeMeulemeester has scored big ..." – *Vancouver Sun*

"Cat is an engaging heroine, and Grimoire
has just the right amount of evil ..."
– *January Magazine*

"... a winning, fun and spooky series."
– *Montreal Review of Books*

"DeMeulemeester does an impressive job of weaving in
sports, academics, an entertaining cast of characters, along
with authentic Celtic fairy lore. Sookie's character is
deliciously eerie ... and Cat's character is truthful and feisty
without being brazen ..." – *CM: Canadian Review of Materials*

Visit the official **"Grim Hill"** series website:
www.grimhill.com

For my own younger brothers and sisters:
Ron, Lezlee, Randy, and Louise

Acknowledgements:
Thank you to Meghan Nolan for her insightful editing and to John Shroades for the wonderful cover – again you've helped me pull together another Grim Hill. And thank you to the staff at Lobster Press for working so hard to get Grim Hill out. Much appreciation to John, Alec, and Joey for their continued support, and to my two nieces, Amanda and Emily, for their fashion advice.

– Linda DeMeulemeester

Grim Hill
The Forgotten Secret

written by
Linda DeMeulemeester

Lobster Press ™

CHAPTER 1

A Wistful Wish

"YOU'RE NOT PLAYING as a team," Mr. Morrows said as he glared at us. "Ever since we joined the boys and girls together as a co-ed soccer team, you've been playing *against* each other instead of *with* each other."

"That's because the guys hog the ball," I said in a huff.

Mia joined in. "Cat's right. I'm the forward and nobody kicks the ball to me."

"Then you'd better move faster," said Mitch as he snatched the soccer ball from Mia's hand and spun it on his fingertips.

"You're the team captain," I said to Clive, hiding the longing in my voice. After all, the position of captain was supposed to have been mine. "Do something about them." I pointed to Mitch, who rolled the soccer ball across the polished gym floor to Zach, who then kicked the ball up and caught it in his hands.

"It's survival of the fittest," Clive, my arch rival, said as he flashed an annoying grin.

Didn't those guys learn anything about how important it is to pull together? I thought we'd discovered at Christmas how to be a team. We'd come together to save the town from Fairy and the evil creatures buried deep beneath Grim Hill. But now everyone else had forgotten about that. The boys still thought they were the only ones going to the intramurals and that the girls were nothing but irritating tag-alongs.

Echoing my thoughts, Emily shook her head saying, "Some co-ed team this is – it's still them against us."

"My point exactly," said Mr. Morrows. "So your coach Ms. Dreeble and I have come to a conclusion."

Ms. Dreeble adjusted the elastic in her blond ponytail and a serious expression crossed her face. My heart sped up as a worry erupted inside me. What if they pull us from the intramurals? What if they disband the team and there's no soccer? Any soccer – even soccer with guys who are ball hogs – is better than no soccer at all.

"Ballroom dancing is the answer," announced Ms. Dreeble as she moved to Mr. Morrows's side. "I've done some research, and schools are discovering how enrolling students in dance classes helps young people build team unity and cooperation."

"Of course Darkmont High does not have the budget for expensive dance studio lessons," explained Mr. Morrows. "So instead of soccer, you are all to show up at the usual practice time, and Ms. Dreeble and I will teach you ballroom dancing steps instead."

"You'll learn the waltz and the fox-trot – maybe even the rumba if there's time." Ms. Dreeble tapped her foot on the floor in four-four time as if she couldn't wait to begin.

My mouth dropped open. Absolute silence hung over all of us in a shroud of gloom until the soccer ball dropped and rolled *clickity-clack* across the gym.

No soccer practice? *Ballroom dancing?*

"But that's a terrible idea," I finally burst out, scowling. How was shuffling around the gym holding some guy's sweaty hand supposed to improve our team cooperation? You can't get better at soccer if you don't practice it.

Sometimes you can see straight through to the point things. Sometimes you can't. I couldn't see the point of dance classes – and it wasn't just me.

Grumbling echoed around the gym as we all turned toward each other. "How will we be ready in time for the competition?" Clive asked bitterly as if he'd just been hit with a soccer penalty. As he leveled me with an angry glare, he added, "It's the girls' fault – they ignore us."

"You mean we don't listen to you," I snapped. "It's *you* guys who ignore *us*."

"Why do you think you are all so special?" Amarjeet shot back at the guys.

"Enough. This is exactly what I mean." Ms. Dreeble's sharp teacher-voice rose above our complaints. "Let me put it this way – we'll have to pull the team out of the competition unless we can get you to play more coopera-tively. So it's your choice – take dance lessons or withdraw from the intramurals."

Okay, I could see *that* point, but everyone was still complaining as dark thundercloud expressions shadowed our teachers' faces. Experience with angry teachers made me figure we were about ten seconds away from having our team withdrawn from the competition. I had to think of something – fast!

I put up my hand.

"Yes, Cat?" Impatience crept into Ms. Dreeble's voice. She thought of me as a bit of a troublemaker and as someone who was not exactly reliable. True, I hadn't shown up for an important soccer game – but in my mind, I had a good excuse. I had been trying to save the town from the perils of Grim Hill.

"What about ..." I said in a loud voice. Everyone got quiet and turned expectantly to me. Ms. Dreeble crossed her arms in a foreboding way, and I could almost smell a detention on the horizon. She looked as if she was in no mood for bargaining. *Think, Cat, think ...*

"What about ... a ... Valentine's dance?"

Complaints turned into murmurs. Hey, maybe I was onto something. Getting into it, I said, "At my old school we had dances all the time. They were really fun." Sure we didn't really dance holding hands with each other. It was more like we all leaped around on the dance floor, spinning like little steel balls bouncing off each other in a pachinko game, but still ... "We have almost three weeks until Valentine's, so we could work hard at our dance lessons and then throw Darkmont's first school dance."

Everyone started saying, "A dance would be cool."

"I'd go to a dance."

"Definitely."

Okay, maybe it was mostly the girls saying this ...

"You're not the ones calling the shots here, Cat," warned Mr. Morrows.

"Although, it might be helpful for you to have a firm goal to work toward," Ms. Dreeble said tentatively.

Was that a glimmer of hope?

"I'm not sure we have money in the budget," Mr. Morrows said as his mustache twitched. Fun was never part of Darkmont's budget. My hope began to sink.

"We have some money left over from the talent

show at Christmas," Ms. Dreeble mused. "But there's not much time."

"I'll help plan," I promised, deciding to jump in before Ms. Dreeble backed out.

"Me too," said Emily, the most popular girl in our grade and also a straight-A student. Even though I too had been considered a good student at my old school, I tried not to let it get to me when Ms. Dreeble only nodded after Emily came on board.

"Okay, we'll have a couple of weeks of dance lessons to build team unity, and you can also sharpen up your cooperation skills by pulling together and planning the Valentine's dance." Ms Dreeble announced this as Mr. Morrows gave her an odd "I wasn't exactly going to agree" look.

It was then I noticed a lot of the guys didn't appear as enthusiastic as the girls. As a matter of fact, they didn't seem interested at all. When our teachers left the gym all the girls gathered into groups and talked excitedly, but the guys still mumbled about soccer being postponed.

"Good one, Cat," complained Clive. "You got us locked up into that one fast."

"You're welcome," I said as sweetly as possible, hoping that would get under his skin. As I walked away, a group of girls signaled me to join them. It was Emily and Amanda and a few of the most popular girls at Darkmont. And *they* wanted to speak to me. Cool.

"We're starting a planning committee right away," Emily said enthusiastically. "We'd like you to join. Great idea you had." Emily shook her blond hair that shone like starlight, even under the dim fluorescent lights. "My mom bought me the most awesome dress for Christmas, and I'll finally have some place in this dingy town to wear it."

"*Ooh*, I hope my mom will get me a new dress," said Amanda. "There's a new designer shop right next to the Emporium. I went in and browsed around over the weekend."

With a distracted smile Emily said, "Maybe once Zach sees me in my dress ..." as she looked over her shoulder watching Clive retreat. It was as if she wouldn't have minded another boy asking her the dance, but everyone assumed the two most popular kids would be a couple. It surprised me to think that just as I felt locked out of getting Zach to ever notice me, maybe Emily felt locked in to going with him because people expected it. "... anyhow, Zach will be happy to take me to the dance." But she didn't sound all that sure of herself.

"Guess I should check out the new store," I said, although I doubted there was money for a new dress in our family budget.

"You'll love those outfits," Amanda said enthusiastically. "Any girl who wears one will be the center of attention at the dance."

She was talking to me like I was part of their crowd. I couldn't believe the popular girls wanted me to join the committee! Okay, maybe the dance was my idea, but still, I'd never been invited to anything by them before. And except for the soccer team we'd begun, Darkmont wasn't exactly loaded with social activities. I'd love to be on the dance committee. This could be my chance to make my life more like it was at my old school, where there were dances and loads of kids to have fun with. Also, it would be great for our soccer team if we all hung out together.

I got that tingling excited feeling from anticipating a great time, so I practically floated out of the school and went straight to the dress shop by the Emporium, even though it was pouring rain outside. An easterly wind had blown in storm clouds, and thunder rumbled in the distance. The rain plastered my hair to my skull, and the chill made my teeth chatter. I didn't care about that as I stood outside Esmeralda's Vintage Designs, because I was mesmerized by the dresses in the window. Inside hung dresses I'd only ever seen in magazines – dresses with ballerina-style skirts and netting that my kid sister would go crazy for, plus silk dresses with lace-up corsets and satin dresses with flouncing skirts, all in frothy sherbet colors of pale lime, strawberry, and blackberry.

Don't get me wrong – I'm no fashionista or anything. I'm more at home in soccer cleats and a tracksuit. It was just that in my old town, even before I'd turned thirteen, I always needed a dress – I'd get invited to all the dances and parties. And my parents had bought me a really nice outfit, although it would never fit now.

I wanted my old life back. Maybe it couldn't be with my dad or my old friends, or my nice house where Mom didn't always have to try to make ends meet. That didn't mean I couldn't have a more fun life here, except … I shook my head and drops of rain flung about, sending extra chills down my face and neck. My hopefulness began washing away in the rain as the grey day seeped inside me. At Christmas when life really started going my way and I'd made team captain, it all got wrecked because of fairy trouble on Grim Hill.

I stared at those dresses thinking *they* seemed right out of a fairy tale – the kind of fairy tale that began "Once upon a time" or "A long time ago." The last thing you want is a real fairy story beginning right here and right now. Trust me on this. Constant danger lurks when you live below a fairy hill. That's another thing – real fairy tales don't wind up happily ever after. You don't meet a prince or find a pot of gold; your troubles don't vanish – not by a long shot. Fairies were pure menace and fairy encounters were perilous!

To make it worse, only our friends the elderly Greystone sisters, my sister Sookie, and our friend Jasper understood that a dark evil lurked inside Grim Hill. Lucinda and Alice Greystone realized this because Lucinda and her soccer team had a run-in with those evil fairies seventy years ago. She had stayed locked up inside the hill until she was an old lady. Because we had feathers I'd taken from Fairy, Jasper, Sookie, and I remembered how twice a terrifying bewitchment fell over our town. The feathers helped us recall what had happened even though no adults or the rest of our soccer team ever remembered. But the feathers weren't entirely reliable – they didn't seem to keep my little sister away from magic, even though she remembered the trouble she'd caused. And that was one other worry that hovered over me.

I didn't want to worry anymore. I wanted to be the girl at the Valentine's dance in the cool dress with lots of friends and all of us having an awesome time. Was that so much to ask?

This time was going to be different!

I tugged on the door of the dress shop.

Maybe I could have a happily ever after at last. Finally we'd locked those wicked fairies inside Grim Hill for good.

Hadn't we?

CHAPTER 2
What an Easterly Wind Blows In ...

THE BELL CHIMED on the door as I entered Esmeralda's shop. A woman bustled in my direction, offering me a towel and taking my jacket so I didn't drip water on any of the fancy tapestry rugs covering the dark wood floor. She wore a suit and her hair was a helmet of hairspray.

"Please, come in and look around," she said, eyeing my muddy shoes with a slight frown. I wiped them again on the bristle mat.

The walls in the shop were covered with delicate rose paper, and the air even smelled like rose petals. This was the fanciest store I'd ever seen – nothing like Mr. Keating's hodgepodge of an Emporium. I moved around uncomfortably, worried I'd knock over a china vase or tip a silk lampshade. Somehow I didn't think a dress from here would be exactly affordable. Maybe there was a sale rack.

Then I spotted *it*. My dream dress.

The shade of the dress wasn't little-girl pink or cotton-candy pink; it was an amazing metallic pink that shimmered in the light. It had grown-up spaghetti straps and a tulip skirt that billowed and dropped above the knees. And it was my size. I walked over and touched it.

"Ah," said the woman. "I see you have excellent taste. This dress is the nicest one here." The woman stared at me – or more like at my tracksuit, and suddenly I was aware how it had faded and pilled up a bit.

I tried to keep my expression casual as I checked out the price tag dangling from the dress strap, but my eyes almost dropped out of my head and rolled onto the floor anyway.

A hundred and eighty dollars!

The cost might as well have been two thousand dollars for all the chance I had of buying it. I backed away and went straight for the door, grabbing my jacket from the fancy brass coat stand. The woman didn't seem surprised. Before I'd even zipped up my coat, I flung open the door as the bell clanged as if to say, "Get out of here!" and I rushed out into the gloom.

When I got home I checked my closet, but my old dress wasn't hanging there. I searched my dresser drawers.

"Mom," I called downstairs. "What happened to my nice dress?"

"And hello to you too," Mom called back. "Ask Sookie."

Before I could step out of my room, Sookie appeared at my door with her hamster, Buddy, gently cradled in the crook of her arm. "It's *my* dress now," Sookie said in a possessive way. "It's in *my* closet."

"You're way too small for it," I said as I shook my head. "You won't fit into it until you're at least eleven, so it's still mine for two more years."

Sookie crossed her arms and huffed, "But Mom said – "

"Fine," I cut her off. I had to approach this differently. Sookie was stubborn. "Can I borrow it for a school dance? It's not like you'll be needing it anytime soon."

Sookie's expression brightened and she said, "Sure, Cat."

Once I tried it on though, she looked at me and said, "I don't think it does you justice." She shook her head sadly.

I couldn't zip it up and it tugged horribly at the shoulders. There was no way this dress would work for the dance.

"Dinner's in ten minutes," Mom said as she walked into Sookie's room. "And Buddy's not invited. He has to have his dinner in the hamster cage." She took one look at the clothes and toys scattered as if a tornado had swept through, and she raised her eyebrows. But she didn't complain. "What's up with you two?" she asked, seeing me shrink-wrapped in the bright blue dress two sizes too small.

"Our school's having a dance," I mumbled, thinking, *Great, Cat, once more you've come up with a way to make your life even more miserable.* It wasn't just that this dress looked horrible on me – I couldn't even move in it.

"Hmm … " Mom started checking the seams and zipper. "Maybe I could let this out some."

"No!" squealed Sookie. "Then I'll never fit into it."

"There's probably not a big enough hem." Mom and Sookie fussed as I just stood there thinking it wasn't a very sophisticated color anyway.

"Maybe I could buy some new material." Mom got that worried tone in her voice again. "How long before the dance?"

"Valentine's," I said shrugging my shoulders. "It's

not a big deal."

"Does it have to be a dress? Maybe I could make you a more practical outfit," Mom said. "A skirt and top that you could wear on more occasions."

"That could work," I said, thinking that wasn't what I wanted at all.

***

Over the weekend I rode my bike past Esmeralda's shop three times and stared at that dress through the window. It was weird, but I saw it as a ticket back to my old life. The third time, I spotted some of the girls, Amanda included, looking at the dresses. I saw Amanda jump for joy when her mother nodded at a really exquisite red dress, even after she saw the price tag. I left before they spotted me.

Shaking my head, I realized how stupid I was. A dress doesn't make you cool or popular. The other girls wouldn't care if my outfit wasn't from that shop, would they? I wondered what Mia and Amarjeet were going to wear. Besides, if Mom wanted to make me a nice new outfit, I should be happy that it would be the kind of thing I could wear often ... except ...

I sighed and rode my bike home, trying to get that dress out of my mind. As I crossed the street ready to turn down my block, I spotted a moving van. Someone new was moving into town.

A red-haired girl – not strawberry blonde like my friend Mia's hair, but a deep auburn that seemed to glow like burning embers – hauled a battered suitcase up the sidewalk. She seemed around my age, and I supposed Darkmont would be getting a new student. The girl smiled at me with lips so red they seemed startling against her milk-white skin, then she slipped behind the door of the ugliest house in the neighborhood. It was a rundown place that had sat empty for ages – long before my mom, sister, and I had moved to this town.

What a strange contrast, I thought as I hopped off my bike. That girl didn't look at all like someone who would live in a place like that. For one thing, her clothes looked expensive and elegant. It was almost as if she was in one of those kid's picture books where you had to find what doesn't belong.

Small shivers raised bumps on my arms. Maybe I was getting chills because one side of the house was next to a cemetery, and the other side was covered in the dark shadow of Grim Hill. But I laughed at myself for being paranoid and then got back on my bike to ride home.

"There's a new girl in our neighborhood," I announced as I strode into the kitchen. "You know that old house on the next street over?"

Sookie was making herself a bowl of frosty oats as an after-school snack. Mom intercepted the cereal box before Sookie poured heaps in her bowl. "You'll spoil your appetite for dinner."

Sookie looked mournful as she dug into the pitiful-looking pile of oats in her bowl. "Who would want to move into that decrepit house across the lane?" She shook her head. "It's inhospitable."

Even though Sookie was only nine, her vocabulary was bigger than mine. Come to think of it, the words she used were bigger than those of any eighth-grader I knew.

"You shouldn't describe a person's house that way," said Mom. "We don't exactly live in a mansion."

Mom sounded like she was saying more than, "Don't judge people." Although she never talked about it, I could tell she still felt bad we'd had to move from our own much nicer home to this old house. We weren't exactly well-off ever since our parents divorced.

"Oh. I'm sorry I called the house decrepit." Sookie hung her blond head, but only for a moment. Then it bobbed up again and with widened eyes she explained, "The kids in my class say that place is haunted, and my friend Skeeter says he thinks he saw a witch in the window yesterday after school."

"A witch ... hardly. You've really got it wrong this time." I loved it when I could feel superior to my little sister. I didn't get the chance very often. And maybe that wasn't nice, but it only seemed fair. I *was* the oldest. "A girl my age moved in. I saw her down the street a few minutes ago and she didn't look like a ghost or a witch." Except the whole moment had given me a chill ... sort of ...

But that was just me getting all worked up because I was letting what happened before on Grim Hill get in the way. Well, those nasty creatures were locked up tight, and I wasn't going to let those stupid fairies in Grim Hill get to me anymore. So I forgot about the creepy house and the girl ... that is, until Monday at school.

A bunch of kids from both soccer teams were hanging out by my friend Jasper's locker. All the girls had been going on and on about the dance when Clive said, "Don't you get it? We're going to be stuck for two weeks wasting our time on dance lessons just as every other soccer team in the competition gets two extra weeks of practice in. The dance only makes it worse."

"It doesn't make it worse," Amarjeet almost shouted. "How does it make it worse? We have to have dance lessons no matter what, so why not have an event to look forward to? Right, Cat?"

The dance had lost some of its excitement for me over the weekend, especially since there was no way I could get a new dress. Besides, I *was* kind of worried about not practicing soccer. Not that Clive needed any encouragement by me agreeing with him. But I nodded half-heartedly and said, "Uh huh."

"C'mon, Cat, be more enthusiastic," Mia whispered to me. "We're having a tough enough time convincing the guys as it is."

"Really?" I asked Jasper. "The guys aren't interested in the dance?"

"Well ..." said Jasper. "It's just ..." I knew Jasper well and there was something worrying him.

But before he said anything, Clive leapt in. "Chung is right. He knows no one needs this distraction."

"I can speak for myself," Jasper pointed out. Except he didn't. He just kept staring at Mia who was glaring at Mitch. Maybe I knew what was bugging him after all. If there was a dance, would Mia dance with him?

Amanda and Emily strolled up just then. Emily said to Zach, "You're interested in the dance, aren't you?"

Zach looked at the other guys and shuffled his feet before saying, "Not exactly ..."

Emily stared at Zach before saying in a surprised

voice, "Seriously?" She seemed dismayed as if him not falling all over her made her think twice that maybe she did like him after all.

Amanda jumped in with, "I'm sure *some* of you guys would like to dance with us, right?" as she tossed her hair over her shoulders. But none of the guys stepped up to the plate. Most of the girls began to glare at them.

"Dancing stinks," complained Clive.

"Just don't mention that to the teachers," I warned. Didn't those boys realize we were about to end up without any soccer team at all if we weren't cooperative? I fumed all the way up to science class.

In class, a firm knock rattled on the door. At first Ms. Dreeble ignored it as she finished writing her question on the board. Someone knocked again, only this time more softly – less sure. With a flip of her wrist, Ms. Dreeble pointed for Mitch to open the door. I sat perched on my lab stool as I watched the same red-haired girl I had seen in my neighborhood walk into our class and place her registration slip on Ms. Dreeble's desk.

Suddenly I had a flashback: Five months ago that was me standing uncomfortably in front of the room – the new kid, looking out at a sea of disinterested faces. That was pretty much the loneliest feeling a person could have.

"Name?" Ms. Dreeble asked.

"Lea," said the girl in a soft, lyrical voice.

"Full name – spell it, please." Ms. Dreeble sounded annoyed. Funny, I knew Ms. Dreeble wasn't really unkind, but she could be impatient, especially when her lesson was interrupted.

"L-e-a-a-n-n. S-h-e-a," said the girl.

Ms. Dreeble scribbled the name on her register and told the girl to sit down. The girl glanced around the classroom as she tried to find an empty seat. She stood frozen in front of us as she wondered where to sit.

"I said, take a seat," said Ms. Dreeble.

Again it was as if that was me standing there, the new kid at school, the one who felt practically invisible. I got up and tugged a lab stool from the corner of the room and pulled it to our table.

"Sit here," I called to her. She broke into a relieved smile and sat beside me.

"I'm Caitlin, but everyone calls me Cat."

"I have the same thing with my name," she said. "I spell it L-e-a even though it's pronounced like 'Lee.'"

I smiled and said, "Lea, this is Mia and that's – "

"I'm Amanda." She shook Lea's hand and said, "That's the most awesome outfit I've ever seen." That was high praise, because Amanda always wore clothes that looked like they'd been bought the week before, and her shoes always looked brand new. I stared at my own warn-out sneakers and slipped them behind my stool.

"Thanks." Lea was wearing a silky green jacket embroidered with silver moons and stars. She had a matching green skirt. It must have cost a fortune.

For the rest of the class I thought about how the popular girl had taken over and spent the entire hour whispering to the new girl. Ms. Dreeble didn't even get on Amanda's case like she would have with me. Maybe what you wore really did matter. When it was lunch and I went to join Amarjeet and Mia, I spotted Lea sitting beside Amanda at the cool kids' table.

The girls at that table all wore expensive tops and pants and the latest boots and sweaters … not like at our table with me still squirming into some of last year's clothes, and Mia in her sensible skirt and blouse, and Amarjeet who always wore dark long-sleeved T-shirts and dress pants. None of our clothes were exactly the height of fashion. Is that how these things get decided? People couldn't just be friends regardless of what they wore?

But I'd been at this school five months and hardly had any friends. This girl hadn't been at the school for five hours. Even Jasper, who was a year younger than me and kind of nerdy, had been invited into Darkmont's elite group – although he rarely sat with them. He didn't even appreciate it. This wasn't fair.

Then Lea pulled a chair to the table. She gestured to me and said, "Sit here."

CHAPTER 3

A Dark Deal

ME? SIT AT *this* table? I stared at Clive, Emily, Amanda, and Mitch. And Zach – a boy I wished would pay more attention to me. Did I dare join them even though the new girl had invited me? The last time I went to sit down at this table it had been a mistake. They'd really been making space for another girl, and I had gotten flustered and dropped my lunch tray, and everyone laughed and …

"C'mon," Lea smiled. "Everyone's talking about you anyway."

"They are?" I shook my head in confusion.

"We're talking about the dance," Emily said. "We're organizing a decorating committee and we're wondering if – since your old school had lots of dances – you'd have some ideas."

"It's all about converting the gym into a more glamorous place," I said, sliding into the seat as if it was mine all along. This wouldn't be easy – Darkmont was, well, dark and dreary. "For the Valentine's theme we could get red decorations: crepe paper streamers, cardboard hearts, and loads of balloons or something like that to hang from the gym ceiling." I wasn't convinced this would give the gym the transformation it would need.

"You realize our school has no budget and there isn't

much time," warned Amanda.

"Balloons are cheap. And there might be stuff on hand at the school," I said, thinking of the meager supplies in our art department.

"So you're in," said Emily. "You're in charge of decorations."

What just happened? What else did I just get myself into? But still I nodded.

"Try to make the gym into something *magnificent*," said Amanda. "This dance is super exciting – Darkmont has never had a dance." Then the girls at the table broke into descriptions of the awesome outfits they were going to wear, while the guys rolled their eyes and talked about how awful our dance classes were going to be.

"What will you wear?" asked Lea.

"I haven't decided," I said, thinking how the blouse and skirt my mom was planning clearly wouldn't cut it compared to the dresses everyone else had described. "There's a dress in Esmeralda's shop, but it's way too expensive."

"Esmeralda's dresses are all designer fashions," bubbled Amanda. "My dress is breathtaking. You've got to get your dress there."

Suddenly all the girls except Lea began talking at once about how they wanted dresses from that store. Funny, Lea had the most expensive clothes of all of us, but she didn't seem to care about Esmerelda's.

I was still thinking about my dream dress after school during our first dance lesson. That is, until I saw something that drove it completely out of my mind for the next hour. We all stood around the gym staring at a horrific sight. Mr. Morrows and Ms. Dreeble were dancing – together! Every kid's mouth hung open and their faces were frozen in shock as they watched our teachers weave in and out of each other's arms until Mr. Morrows spun Ms. Dreeble around in a pirouette. They laughed and bowed to the class. It was almost too much for the eyes to take. A few kids clapped hesitantly, breaking the awkward silence.

"Now class, I want everyone to choose a partner, and the dance lessons will begin," instructed Ms. Dreeble.

Just when I thought it couldn't get worse. At first we just kind of shuffled around, and I could see I wasn't the only one who found this nerve-wracking. Who would I choose? Zach had already grabbed Emily's hand. Then Clive swaggered forward. He walked toward me. *Keep walking right past me*, I shouted in my mind. As he came closer he began to slow down.

No … noooo … I looked away hoping not making eye contact would render me invisible, but he grabbed my hand anyway. Should I have been flattered? Hardly. He used this time to complain about how these lessons would ruin soccer. Dark tornados swirled above my head as I listened.

Finally I said, "Look, it wasn't my idea of the dance that made the teachers decide on these lessons. It was vice versa."

"Your bright idea didn't help," was his angry reply. I watched everyone else get into pairs and thought, *Why couldn't I have chosen one of* those *boys first*. Any other boy would have been better! Why had I hesitated … but I knew the answer. Because the boy I would have chosen had picked another girl.

While we all stood facing each other but not exactly looking directly at each other, Ms. Dreeble blew her whistle. "Okay everyone, listen and watch. Boys follow Mr. Morrows's example and put your right foot forward, then slide together, step and slide together, step."

The boys dragged their feet as they tried to follow Mr. Morrows. "Girls, now it's your turn." This time Ms. Dreeble demonstrated her version of slide-together-step. It didn't seem too hard.

"Now together with your partner." As Ms Dreeble ran around placing our hands over the boys' shoulders and the boys' hands on our backs, I wanted to pull my own hand away as if it was burnt. Even Clive only put his hand near my back, keeping space between my sweater and his fingers. Our hands slid around because both our palms were sweaty. Ballroom dancing looked way better on television. In real life, it was pretty gross.

Mr. Morrows put on a song that he called "Moonlight Serenade." It was a song my mother would consider old-fashioned. I bet it was a song even a grandmother would think wasn't cool. A few moments later I totally understood the saying, "Getting off on the wrong foot."

"Ouch!" Clive complained. "You just stomped on my foot."

"Well you put it under *my* foot," I shot back.

"That's because I'm supposed to lead, not you."

"Says who?" I stopped and put my hands on my hips.

"Says tradition," said Ms. Dreeble, the last person I thought would support guys going first. She got upset when she had told us about all the early women scientists who had to fight men for very little recognition. I thought she wouldn't quibble over who got to step forward and who was to step back. "The boy leads, Cat."

Fine. With forced enthusiasm I took a huge step backward, only to tangle my feet into the couple behind us. Mitch shoved me forward and I fell onto Clive, catching him off guard. We both tumbled to the floor.

Everyone laughed including me, but Clive picked himself up and stormed off. Great. Then Ms. Dreeble walked up to me, and I could see detention brewing in her eyes.

"Sorry," I said meekly. But she simply shook her head. I stood alone in the middle of the gym floor as the rest of the class continued practicing the fox-trot. I noticed that none of the other boys rushed over to be my partner.

***

Later, Jasper waited for me by my locker and we walked home together. All the way home, I went on about the dress at Esmeralda's shop and how much it cost, but when I asked Jasper if he had any brainstorms for raising money he just ignored me.

Instead he said, "I hate our teachers' idea of dance lessons – how come you're into it? Clive said you're even in charge of decorations."

"It's a way to get everyone cooperating. Otherwise, our teachers will pull us from the intramurals," I protested. "I just thought a dance would be cool if we had to have the lessons anyhow."

Jasper looked sort of uncomfortable and his face

reddened a little when he said, "Do you think we're supposed to have ... dates?"

Dates. My heart thudded...I hadn't thought of that. At my old school we would all just show up. But that was a year ago, and we were all kids then. Was a date a requirement of being a high-schooler? Maybe. I was really going to need that dress so I could brag about it at lunch, and then maybe I'd find a date. Clearly I hadn't thought out the details. *First things first*, I told myself and promptly returned to my original question. "Hey, so what kinds of jobs do you think a thirteen-year-old can get?"

Jasper shrugged his shoulders and suggested, "What about babysitting?"

"No good, Emily and Amarjeet have all the regular babysitting jobs in town."

"And I've got the only paper route," he said. "Why do you want the *most* expensive dress in the shop?"

Why? Because it was amazing. I couldn't explain it, but it was just the right dress – nothing else compared. "I need a job," I said stubbornly. The shadows along the streets deepened, and the streetlights flickered on. A quiet gloom gathered in the air as the sun set, and I longed for spring and longer days. Jasper and I picked up our pace until I saw a flash of white out of the corner of my eye.

It was the new girl, Lea. She was leaning over her fence and waving to us with a pale white hand. We turned down her road.

"Hi," she said as she smiled, and a small voice in my head was saying, *This girl could be a good friend*. "Are you just getting back from school?"

"Dance lessons." I made a face and Jasper scowled.

"Right," she nodded sympathetically. "So have you decided what dress you're going to pick for the dance?"

"I have," I said.

"She just has to afford it." Jasper shook his head. "It costs a fortune."

"Maybe I'll get some odd jobs," I mused.

"Someone's looking for a job?" A voice came from the side of Lea's yard, and an attractive woman with long blond hair and dressed in a grey gardening smock came up to the fence. Skeeter was crazy. If he'd seen this woman in the window, how could he think she was a scary witch? He had some imagination – she was stunning.

"I need a lot of help digging my garden plot. I'll hire you. I'll pay both of you if you're interested in working here on Saturday."

"Really? It's a deal. I'm Cat and …"

The woman waved her gardening gloves. "Sweetie, I've already heard a lot about you."

"You have?" I said, puzzled.

"Both from Lea and a little cutie named Sookie. Your mother and sister came over earlier to welcome us. Why don't you come by later tonight, and we'll work out the details."

"Sounds like a plan," I said with enthusiasm.

"Isn't it early for gardening?" asked Jasper. "We still get a lot of frost and maybe some snow at the beginning of February."

Thanks, Jasper, I thought with a touch of annoyance. But the woman simply said, "My plants are special."

That seemed odd to say. I had a sudden image of a bumper sticker that said, "My carrots are on the honor roll," and I couldn't hide my smile. Jasper couldn't make it tonight; he had to work at his parents' restaurant, but he said he'd be there Saturday.

We both said goodbye to Lea, but as I turned to wave I noticed that as Grim Hill's shadows swallowed the ground, Lea's rickety house seemed full of dark creepy corners.

It did look haunted.

CHAPTER 4

A Diabolical Match

AFTER DINNER, I stood on the dilapidated porch of Lea's old house as the shrill wind rattled the upstairs shutters until they banged back and forth against the window pane. Not even a sliver of light escaped from the heavy dark drapes in the front window. The inky sky somehow seemed blacker above the house because Grim Hill loomed behind. I hesitated before I lifted the old iron doorknocker. I'd learned to trust the icky feeling I sometimes got on the back of my neck.

"What are you waiting for?"

Oh, and I was stuck with my little sister who didn't seem one bit uneasy. Mom was at the school this evening. The city college held continuing education classes there, and Mom had signed up for one. She wanted to finish her degree and get a better-paying job. So if I wanted to hang out with Lea, I had to bring along Sookie, which was going to put a serious damper on me appearing even a little bit cool.

The peculiar doorknocker was shaped like a dog's head, and not the cute puppy type. A brass green snarling beast had a ring through his nose that clanged against his pointy fangs and echoed when I knocked, as if the whole house was an empty cavern on the inside. We stood for a while on the porch, and finally we heard the slow footsteps of someone approaching and the sound of a bolt slamming back.

For a fleeting second I had the impulse to grab my sister's hand and run. You could never be too careful in a town like this, where evil had a way of finding its way out of Grim Hill. Luckily I stayed put because when the door cracked open, yellow light splashed out and we were greeted by Lea's smile that was just as bright.

"I'm glad you made it." Lea was dressed in a jade jacket with gold dragonflies embroidered along the sleeves. I'd never seen such an awesome top. She invited us in, and when I took off my red jacket, I brushed the fuzzy flecks off my black turtleneck sweater and tried to straighten a few wrinkles out my jeans.

When I looked up, my mouth dropped open. The inside of Lea's house was like the inside an exotic tent. Bead curtains hung from all the doorways, and silk drapes colored the walls and ceiling. Old-fashioned glass lamps were fastened against a wall and they glowed like torches.

"Cool house," was all I managed to say. I could see I was making a brilliant impression.

Lea smiled again, but her smile faded when someone from behind me said, "Well if it isn't our new neighbors." It was my future employer, greeting us. It made me think about how my mother always said people were too quick to make judgments. I mean, just because Lea and her aunt had to live in a house that needed a lot of work, Skeeter and Sookie had assumed it was a haunted place. That wasn't fair. Look how nice the house was on the inside! And they were both so welcoming.

"I didn't introduce you before. This is my aunt Bea,"

Lea said to me, but her voice sounded flat – almost worried.

Lea and her aunt had rhyming names. Was it a family thing? "Hi … um … Ms. – "

"Just 'Bea' is fine," she said as she took my hand and shook it. Her hand felt cold. I guessed the house was extremely drafty. Come to think of it, I felt a definite chill as I stood in the hall, and my scalp tingled, almost as if someone – or something – was brushing against my hair.

"For my old friend Sookie," Bea joked, "I have some plants and seedlings for you to take home to your mother. Would you like to come see?"

Sookie nodded eagerly and got a glint in her eye that I hadn't seen since Jasper and I gave her … the magic kit! I grew uneasy when she disappeared into the back of the house with Bea.

"Want to check out my room?" asked Lea.

"Sure, in a second. I just want to make sure Sookie doesn't, um, drive your aunt crazy. My sister can be a little intense..." That was my excuse as I followed my sister and Lea's aunt and watched as they began an animated conversation over the potted plants on the back porch.

"What kind of plant is this?" Sookie asked eagerly.

"Ragwort," said Lea's aunt. "In the old days they said witches used it for transporting souls." Then Bea laughed, but it wasn't a dismissive chuckle. It was a deep belly laugh – as if she thought what she'd said was hilarious. "It's poisonous, so no touching it or pulling off the leaves. I keep it locked behind a gate so cats and curious children keep away. But I like it because it grows easily in any soil – like a weed."

"Ooh, it has such a pretty flower." Sookie's eyes

flashed with interest. "What plant is this?"

"Yew," said Bea. "In times past, it was grown in graveyards. The roots were supposed to keep the dead from wandering the world."

"That's gruesome," Sookie said with utter enthusiasm.

That seemed like a pretty weird collection of plants, and I didn't exactly like the twinkle in Sookie's eyes as she hovered over them. Then Lea grabbed a branch and handed it to Sookie.

"Forget about those nasty weeds," Lea said. "Here's a nicer plant – yarrow. If you cut the stem and place it under your pillow before you go to sleep, in the morning you will see the initials of your true love."

"Yuck," said Sookie, finally horrified.

"Are there any other plants to help in the love department?" I asked, thinking about the Valentine's dance and how Jasper wanted to ask Mia, but she only cared about Mitch.

Lea shrugged her shoulders. "Lavender, I think." She pointed to the stick-like grass in a yellow pot.

Sookie rolled her eyes. Bea whispered something about "twitch grass" to Sookie, and my sister laughed as goose bumps walked up and down my arms. I was relieved when everyone stopped talking about the plants.

"Sookie, would you like some hot chocolate?" suggested Lea.

"Sure," my sister said and we went back into the kitchen. Bea started heating some milk.

"I'll make you two some as well," Bea offered. She sounded so nice my nerves settled back down as Sookie studied a tray, deciding which cup would hold the most hot chocolate.

"Can we go check out your room now?" I said to Lea.

We climbed the massive oak staircase to the second floor. I couldn't believe it. Lea had a canopied bed – something I'd always wanted! She also had a big fireplace in her own bedroom and there was a fire crackling inside it. As if my mother would ever let me have an unattended fire in my room! Along the wall was a big bookcase filled with books. Imagine not having to go to the library every time you wanted something to read. You could take as long as you wanted with a book and never have to worry about overdue fines.

As I admired the titles I said, "Wow, you sure have a great collection – Jasper would be totally envious." Although as I glanced around, I had to admit he wouldn't be the only one.

"There's no reason to envy me," Lea said. "When you change schools all the time, books are your only close friends." Lea flipped a strand of red hair behind her ear, revealing a long dangling earring of sparkling green stones. Dangling earrings – this girl was so sophisticated, as if she was sixteen. "My aunt and I move around a lot."

"I know how that feels." I was remembering my first day at Darkmont back in September. Changing schools was hard. As Sookie so perfectly explained it, my first day had been ghastly. "It's like when you move to a new place, you have to prove yourself all over again."

"And no one really understands you." Lea hung her head.

"Exactly," I sympathized. "I never feel like people

get who I really am."

Lea brightened and said, "Seems like we have a lot in common."

"It's true," I said, although I wasn't as sure. I swept an admiring glance at her closet filled with clothes, and at her desk, which held a basket of silver bangle bracelets, and an entire row of nail polish bottles.

"Would you like to borrow some nail polish?" Lea asked, noticing my lingering glaze.

"No, that's okay." I didn't want Lea thinking I just liked her for her stuff. Besides, my mother wouldn't let me wear nail polish anyway.

"No seriously, try this shade. It doesn't really work for me because of my hair color."

Lea chose a metallic pink nail polish, the exact shade of the dress I was hoping for. She handed me the bottle. I tried to give it back – I knew I should give it back – but the color was so perfect.

"Look," Lea said reaching into a drawer. "I have a scarf the same color. Again, it's a shade I shouldn't really wear."

The scarf was as crinkly and airy as tissue and the light shone right through making the soft pinks shimmer. Lea held the scarf against me. "It looks amazing against your dark hair." She gently shoved me toward a mirror. "Also, it tones down your, um, green highlights."

She was right. With the scarf tied around my neck, the green streaks in my hair that I was stuck with since my first fairy encounter didn't look half bad. "Wow. Thanks," I said, realizing that a friendship can't be all one way. As I wondered what I could do for Lea in return, her aunt called up for us to join them in the kitchen.

Downstairs, Sookie was slurping her hot chocolate. "This is really good," she said to me. "What's in this?"

"I've grated in some peppermint from my herb garden," said Bea. She handed me a mug. "Here, I made peppermint mochas for you and Lea."

Mocha. My mother was very stingy about doling out any coffee. As a matter of fact, I'd only had one latte in my entire life. I took a sip of Bea's homemade mocha.

"Thank you, this is delicious."

"Sure. Okay, so let's see ... about Saturday, the digging is going to be a big job," said Bea. "So you might want to bring another person besides that young man I met earlier."

I looked at Lea feeling a bit selfish. Bea had asked me to find extra helpers, but Lea might want to ask Emily or Amanda. I wasn't ready to lose my new friend to the most popular girls in school.

"What about Clive?" I suggested. It occurred to me that he was so annoying, I doubt he'd win anyone away from me.

Lea's face darkened, and I worried I was doing something that made her unhappy. But then she said, "Sure."

Before I could figure out what I'd said, Sookie, not wanting to be left out asked, "Can I help? Can I bring a friend?"

My little sister never seemed to get the fact that we weren't equals – that I'd had to earn my privileges. She always expected the exact same treatment.

"That would be lovely," said Lea's aunt with a smile.

Sookie seemed oblivious to my glare. After finishing my mocha, I helped my sister gather the plants that Bea was sending to my mother. Of course, Sookie managed to talk Lea's aunt into providing a couple of plants for herself as well. It was probably for the best. My mother didn't exactly have a green thumb, although if these plants could resist the cold, maybe my mother wouldn't kill them too quickly.

"See you Saturday," I told Lea, her nail polish and scarf tucked into my pocket. "Thank you," I mouthed. She nodded and managed a smile. Maybe I'd misread her before. She no longer looked upset.

I wondered if working part-time and becoming friends with Lea would make my mom finally see that I was getting older and should be able to have some of the privileges that Lea had. I could be trusted to be more responsible.

As my sister and I stepped into the yard, wind chimes out back made a whispering sound. I swear they were saying, "Beware."

CHAPTER 5

Shadows from the Past

ON MY WAY to school the next morning, I stopped at Mr. Keating's Emporium and asked him if I could put a flyer in the window. It read:

> *No job too big – no job too small.*
> *If there's a garage to clean,*
> *Or a yard to preen,*
> *Give Cat Peters a call.*

I thought it was pretty catchy. Sookie had helped me with the word to rhyme with clean. She assured me it fit. I'd also cut and pasted a border with garden shears, brooms, dust mops, and shovels – all in color. Soon I'd be earning enough money for the dress. Mr. Keating was dragging out his apple barrel. I ran over and gave him a hand.

"I'm quite behind this morning, Cat. I don't suppose you could help me carry a couple of other vegetable boxes out as well."

"Sure thing," I said.

In a flash I carried a box of potatoes and two boxes filled with carrots, and placed them on the bench at the front of the store. "Anything else?" I asked. Before he could answer, I added, "You know, I come by here every

44

morning. If you were looking for a part-time worker who could set up the vegetables under your awning and stock some shelves, I could do it."

Mr. Keating looked thoughtful. "Could you be here an hour earlier every day?"

I wasn't exactly a morning person, but I nodded enthusiastically. "Absolutely."

"Monday through Saturday, an hour each day. I'll pay you fifty dollars a week."

I wasn't crazy about waking up so early on a Saturday morning, but this job would give me more than one hundred dollars by the time of the dance! "Okay, it's a deal. Thanks!"

I helped bring out two more boxes of turnips and onions and wondered if he'd include today's time in my paycheck. Afterward, I stopped in front of Esmeralda's window and admired my dress. I adjusted Lea's pink scarf that I'd tied around my neck and wondered how it would look draped around that dress. I wiggled my toes in my running shoes, reminding myself that I'd used Lea's nail polish and painted them the same shimmering pink as the dress. I'd left my fingernails plain – no sense flashing the nail polish right under Mom's nose. I'd ask her when the mood was right.

I hurried to school, but I was late. I must have sounded sincere when I explained to Ms. Dreeble I'd just started a part-time job and would leave home earlier from now on, because she just nodded and said, "Okay."

In science class I couldn't help staring at Ms. Dreeble as she lectured about plants. She looked so different, and it took me a moment to figure out why. Ms. Dreeble was wearing new ultra-cool glasses and without her thick lenses and old-fashioned frames, she looked a lot different. Then I realized her hair wasn't pulled back in a ponytail either. Instead she wore it loose and it curled softly around her shoulders.

"Cat, could you explain to us the difference between a symbiotic and a parasitic relationship?"

For a second I wondered if she was talking about the way she changed her appearance right after she and Mr. Morrows had danced together – then I realized the question must have had something to do with her lecture. I fiddled with my pen.

Amanda frantically waved her hand. This didn't seem right. Clearly she *had* the answer, so why was Ms. Dreeble picking on me?

"Fine. Amanda?" Ms. Dreeble said as she gave me a cold stare that wasn't quite as unsettling as when she used to peer over her old glasses. "What can you tell me about those two relationships?"

"A symbiotic relationship is mutually beneficial," droned Amanda. "A parasitic relationship is harmful to the host."

"Well done," said Ms. Dreeble. "Cat, can you give us examples of those relationships from the plant kingdom."

My heart thudded in my chest. I thought I'd gotten off the hook. I had no idea. Lea was trying to mouth a word to me, but I was distracted because Amanda was waving her arm around again.

Ms. Dreeble motioned for Amanda to wait. "Then how about giving us an example of those relationships from the animal kingdom?"

Again all I could think about was glasses and lenses ... no ponytails ... teachers who danced together – what was the relationship there? I shook my head.

Amanda was waving her arm so hard I thought it might dislocate from her shoulder.

"Cat, I want you to write me a paragraph on those relationships, and use examples from both the plant and animal kingdom. I'd like it on my desk by next Monday." The bell rang and class was dismissed.

"What were you trying to say to me?" I asked Lea as she walked with me.

She flashed a smile and said, "I whispered 'symbiotic' – because I think we're very symbiotic."

For a moment I was puzzled, and then I said, "You mean we have a friendship that's mutually beneficial?"

"Exactly," Lea said and smiled, then she hurried to her next class.

I stood in the darkened hall of Darkmont for a minute. I didn't think that answer would have gotten me off the hook with Ms. Dreeble, but still, I was flattered.

At lunch, I vented to Mia and Amarjeet as we stood by my locker. "Seriously, Ms. Dreeble totally has it in for me."

"Everyone says their teachers have it in for them when they get caught daydreaming," said Mia pulling markers out of her locker. I'd talked her into joining the decorating committee with me. We were going to make posters during lunch for the dance.

"C'mon, Amarjeet, help us out with the posters," pressured Mia.

"What's the point? Do you think I'll ever get Rabinder to notice me?" They both started complaining about how they didn't think either of the boys they liked would actually go with them to the dance.

My soccer friends didn't seem to care about how Ms. Dreeble was always on my case. Impatiently, I said to Amarjeet, "The bell will ring in twenty minutes and we need to get these posters done and then check out the art room for supplies. Are you coming or not?"

"Wow, Cat, just because you sit at the table with all your new friends, doesn't give you the right to get bossy with us." Amarjeet said as she stormed away.

Whoa, where did that come from? Besides, I'd only sat at that table for about fifteen minutes as I gulped down my lunch and brainstormed decorations for the dance.

"Good one, now it's only us." Mia shook her head as we walked to the art room. I still wasn't sure what I had done.

As we walked along Darkmont's dingy corridor, Lea caught up to us. "Can I come?" she said breathlessly.

"For sure," I said, and Mia nodded enthusiastically.

Darkmont's art room had a huge storage area at the back that looked like it hadn't been cleaned out or dusted in about a hundred years. I started sneezing as soon as we opened the door of the storage area and stared at the long shelves disappearing into the dim light.

"Poster paper is on the shelf back there," Mia pointed, trying to stifle her own sneeze.

Lea raced to the back of the room and grabbed the paper when I spotted a huge box marked "Valentine's." "Look at this. There's got to be some stuff in here we can use." This would be great, because between the dance lessons after school and my part-time jobs, I didn't have a lot of time to get decorations ready for the dance. Funny, although Emily and everyone agreed I'd be perfect for the committee, nobody rose to the occasion *with* me – except for Mia and Lea, that is.

"Hey, there are two more boxes besides that one." Mia started hauling down the first box and Lea grabbed the smaller one. Once we got the boxes out of the storage room and onto the table, I began sneezing again.

Mia brushed a thick layer of dust off the first box. "I think it's been awhile since Darkmont's had a Valentine's dance." She opened the box and pulled out large crimson foil hearts, and then she unpacked rolls of red and white crepe paper.

Opening the second box, I said with delight, "These will look great hanging from the ceiling." I held up beautiful red Japanese silk lanterns – these were just what we needed to transform Darkmont's gym into a more enchanting place.

"What's this?" I picked up the discarded newspaper that had been used to wrap up the hearts. "I think this paper is from a really long time ago. The boy and girl in the picture are dressed in very old-fashioned clothes."

"So what?" Mia shrugged. "The decorations are still in perfect condition." Then as an afterthought she laughed, "Bet that's the last time Darkmont sponsored a school dance."

"Maybe," I agreed, only half-listening as I smoothed the paper out on the table and studied the grainy photograph on the front page. A boy and a girl stood side by side with a few other kids in front of our school. Most of the headline and all of the date had been faded away, but it was something about "boy found ... still missing." The headline was a bit of a puzzle with half of it invisible. I felt heat on the back of my neck, and I turned to see Lea staring intently at the photo. It wasn't *that* interesting ...

"Gross," said Mia. "These decorations smell nasty."

"I guess they're musty. That's typical. There's never money to replace anything that could be fun at this school, so this box has probably sat on the shelf for decades." I began pulling all the decorations out of the box. "We better put them all out on a table and let them air out. I still think they look okay – what do you think, Lea?"

Lea shrugged her shoulders and said, "It's not as if Valentine's has changed much over the years." And then she didn't say anything else.

I guessed that meant they were okay.

All afternoon I couldn't concentrate as I tried to picture the gym and where to hang the red lanterns for the dance, causing Mr. Morrows to ask if I even knew which class I was in. This gave Clive no end of amusement. On the way home from school I walked by Lea's house. I'd hoped I'd run into her hanging out by the gate, but she wasn't outside. It looked like Lea's aunt had already begun to dig her garden, so I opened the gate and walked to the side of the yard to check it out.

Even though it wasn't yet evening, the side yard was darker in the shadow of the hill. Old crumbling pots, a broken bench, and tangles of dead vines added to the gloom. Each freshly dug garden plot was marked by a flat stone, eerily resembling the graveyard next door.

The east wind rose up again and branches rustled and creaked as they brushed by the tin roof of the garden shed. The wind was making a shrill wailing noise. As I crossed the yard and stood at the back of the house, it seemed to me this place would be a perfect setting for a horror movie. I shivered.

A shudder on the second floor banged open. I jumped and when I turned to look I thought I saw a face in the window – an ugly melting face as hideous as a rotting apple. A sharp yelp escaped me and then the image was gone. It must have just been some weird reflection in the window, but the hair on my neck still stood on end and I couldn't wait to get out of there.

I ran back to the side of the yard and headed for the gate. *Coincidence, coincidence*, I chanted to myself as I hurried home. Before I went into my house I walked over to my own backyard that sat at the foot of Grim Hill. Shaking my fist, I shouted to the hill. "I want a happy life. No fairies, no trouble," I yelled. "Stay away!"

The hill stayed silent – no strange whispers, no weird lights – and I got the sense that Grim Hill truly was quiet.

Except even as I let out a sigh of relief, I could still hear the wailing, and this time I wasn't so sure it was the wind.

CHAPTER 6

A Garden of Secrets

AS THE NIGHT settled in and dark gathered around our house, I decided that I'd just felt jittery, that's all. A knot untied in my stomach and I went downstairs for dinner. Mom was rushing out the door for her business class.

"Please go ahead and heat up leftovers for you and your sister. Oh, and Cat …" Mom opened the hall closet and pulled out two bolts of fabric. "I bought this black material for your skirt. So depending on your blouse, it could be quite fancy for a dance and …" Mom smiled as she unfolded a bolt of red satin dotted with tiny green leaves. "How's this? Won't it make a perfect blouse for a Valentine's dance?"

"Great," I said smiling enthusiastically all the while thinking that between the red and green blouse and the green stripes in my hair, I'd look like I was going to a Christmas party instead. "Um … Mom …" But I couldn't bring myself to say I didn't like the outfit and that I really wanted the dress in the store. Instead I said, "I've got a part-time job at the Emporium, just for an hour in the mornings, and I'm going to do some yard work for our new neighbor."

Mom quietly folded the material back in the bag. "That's fine, Cat." Her voice lost some of its enthusiasm and I guiltily noticed she didn't mention the outfit again.

"As long as it doesn't cut into schoolwork." Then she said, "I realize you've been short on spending money."

I mumbled "thanks" and went to heat up dinner.

"Can we go over to Aunt Bea's tonight?" Sookie asked later when we sat down to eat.

"She's not your aunt," I snapped harshly, although I had no idea why.

"Bea told me I could call her that – and Mom doesn't care," Sookie said before chomping into her chicken drumstick. Because Mom had left for school, Sookie's hamster, Buddy, perched on her shoulder while she offered him her carrots. Buddy wasn't exactly welcome at our dinner table, but I didn't feel like more arguing. Besides, with his tiny mouth and delicate nibbles, he somehow seemed more polite than my sister.

"Don't talk with your mouth full," I said automatically.

"You're not the boss," Sookie said intentionally with a mouthful of food.

I sighed. That was the second time today somebody called me bossy. As if being in charge of Sookie was loads of fun. And I still didn't get what Amarjeet was upset about.

"So can we go to Aunt Bea's? I've got lots of questions about those plants she gave me. I'm keeping my plants in pots," Sookie said with authority. "That way the roots stay warmer. And I've put rocks at the bottom for good drainage."

"Whatever ..." I said. "Just don't get too focused on your new gardening hobby." Sookie could get obsessive over stuff, and it usually didn't turn out well.

"Please can we go tonight?" Sookie never gave up.

"Homework," I said.

"Tomorrow?"

"More homework." I didn't want Sookie getting too carried away with her stupid plants. I took my plate and wrapped it in plastic wrap and placed it in the fridge for later. "Don't forget, Mom said to be in bed by eight."

"You never enforce that," complained Sookie.

"Well it's about time you realize you're not old enough for all the things you think you're entitled to, and that includes doing everything I do and staying up late." I slammed the fridge door and went to the study to get an early start on my paragraphs for Ms. Dreeble.

"You're kidding ... right, Cat?" Sookie sounded truly puzzled.

When I banged the door shut to the study she finally got the hint and left me alone. I switched to Google Scholar so the child security lock – thanks for the trust, Mom – on the internet would allow me to visit websites on symbiotic relationships. Then I began reading how it was just like Amanda had been explaining in science class – that symbiotic was when two living organisms from different biological species have a relationship from which they both benefit. Parasitic was when two biological species have a relationship where one species benefits and the other is harmed or even killed.

Okay, so now I was getting an idea about those two terms, but I still needed to find examples for my homework. As I was trying to decide which search engine the computer lock would let me ask my question, there was a soft knock on the front door.

I got up from the study and took a quick look through the window in the front door and saw Lea standing on our porch. Smiling, I yanked open the door and invited her in.

"Hi. I was wondering if you felt like hanging out." She said it a little hopefully.

"Sure," I said, forgetting all about my homework assignment. Besides, there was still the absolute injustice that I was the only student who had to do it. Remembering the mocha we'd had at her place, I asked, "Would you like some coffee?"

Lea nodded enthusiastically, so we went into the kitchen as I tried to figure out how to work the coffee maker – without much success. There were a lot of buttons.

"Maybe if you make instant coffee it will be easier," suggested Lea.

I checked out the cupboard and found a jar of instant coffee and quickly scooped a heaping tablespoon each of the granules into two coffee mugs and set the kettle to boil. When the kettle whistled, I whisked it off the stove. No point alerting Sookie that I had company. The coffee frothed in the cup when I stirred it, and then I placed cream and sugar on the table.

I almost gagged on my first slurp. I sputtered and had to run to the sink. "Watch out, it's a little hot," I said. Then I went back to the table and poured a ton of cream and sugar into my mug. "And it might be a little strong."

"The coffee's fine," said Lea, and she swallowed a big gulp, not minding the burning liquid at all. "I wish I could go to the dance and just chill like a regular kid." Lea couldn't hide the longing in her voice.

My mouth dropped in surprise – that was exactly what I wanted. Except I wasn't sure what *she* meant by "regular." "Why can't you go?"

With a mournful sigh, Lea's mouth turned down as she said, "I guess you could call it a family rule." The way she sat rigid in the chair – tense, as if she might jump up and run – prevented me from asking her what she meant. Bea certainly didn't look strict, and Lea had seemed way ahead of me on privileges. Still we clearly had things in common, so I decided to share some of my troubles.

I told her about my friends at school, and it was as if a dam burst inside me. I mentioned again the dress I desired, about wishing to have more fun at school, about how my friends didn't seem to care when I complained about unfair teachers – not to mention a pesky sister who caused me a lot of trouble. Sure, I left out the bit about how I jumped at every shadow and loud noise and worried if magic might be creeping into our town, but I didn't exactly want to send Lea fleeing into the night to get away from me, the crazy girl.

Lea complained about how she and her aunt never stayed around more than a month or two before they moved on to the next place, and how without any sisters or brothers and no close friends, she lived a solitary life.

I told her she wasn't missing much being constantly pestered by a younger sibling. And my other friends could testify to that. Amarjeet came quickly to mind. Her brother was always spying on her and blackmailing her. But Lea seemed unconvinced.

"I'm bringing another friend on Saturday," I reminded her, although I kept forgetting to ask Clive.

56

"And Sookie's coming, and she's bringing her pesky friend Skeeter." Although secretly I was now happy he was coming – he'd entertain her so I wouldn't have to keep as sharp an eye on her.

Lea brightened at the prospect. "Cool, but you'd all better come around six."

"Huh? It will be dark by then."

"My aunt only works in her garden by moonlight," said Lea. "The daylight triggers her migraines. And Saturday is only a short while after the full moon, so there should still be lots of light."

Speaking of headaches, I was starting to get one, so I put my mug down after drinking only half the coffee.

"About bringing your sister ... I really like her, it's just that I'm not sure ... she seems very ..." Lea paused and tilted her head as if she was listening to something. Then I could hear it too, a soft eerie melody coming from the backyard.

We both got up and went to the back door. I opened it up a crack and we peered out to the patio where Sookie kept her potted plants. The moon glowed softly from the night sky. Moon rays traveled down and pooled like spotlights on the plants and my sister. She was chanting to a plant and cradling it in her hands. I swear the plants had grown about a foot since the other night. Dread seeped right through me. This whole plant thing *wasn't* normal. My head ached and I rubbed my forehead. How did this all fit? My odd chills, these plants ...

Lea pulled me back inside the kitchen and closed the door.

"Your sister is ... unusual," Lea said in a flat voice

that gave me even more shivers of dread. It was almost as if she sensed Sookie's ... strange abilities.

Then as if Lea still read my mind, she said, "Look, that's licorice root she's growing – make sure she doesn't put any in your cereal because it will put you under her power." Lea flashed a half-smile as if to see how I'd react.

I hoped she was joking, but I couldn't exactly say, "Yeah, my sister can get pretty carried away with her magic."

"And the plant she's holding is mullein. It's said when you burn that as incense it can raise the dead."

But then she let out a shaky laugh and though my head began pounding, I managed a giggle too.

Lea's voice drifted as she watched Sookie tenderly dig to loosen the soil in another one of her potted plants. "And that's Spanish moss."

That plant looked creepy in the moonlight – like a mass of grey worms.

"I wonder why my aunt gave your sister those plants ..." Lea looked over her shoulder as if she was expecting someone. "Maybe I'd better go home and see what Aunt Bea is doing," she said nervously.

Lea seemed to be acting a bit strange. I rubbed my aching head and thought that lately that's how everything felt to me. After I walked Lea to the door, I heard Sookie's accusing voice behind me. "You're not allowed to have coffee."

Great. I'd forgotten to wash up the mugs in the kitchen. I glanced nervously at my watch wondering how much time was left before Mom got home. But that wouldn't stop Sookie from telling on me ... unless ...

"And you're not supposed to be practicing magic without Alice and Lucinda's supervision."

"What? What do you mean?" Sookie's voice squeaked in surprise, but she looked positively guilty.

So Sookie knew she was using magic! "I mean," I said sternly, "Your plants are growing like crazy, and I'm guessing you're using more than water and sunlight to accomplish that."

Tears welled in Sookie's eyes, and a single tear spilled down her cheek. "I'm being good, really. No one is whispering to me to make the plants grow – no one is putting ideas into my head. I – I just know that I can do it. I like growing things."

"No magic," I insisted. "Not one drop more until I talk to the Greystones."

I didn't like the stubborn look Sookie got, but she went to bed without another word.

That night a shrill wail cut through to my bones, and it definitely wasn't the wind. I tossed and turned and couldn't sleep, but the coffee wasn't to blame. Between the weird shriek, Sookie's plants, and a jittery feeling I couldn't shake, a dark worry had grabbed hold of my heart and wouldn't let go. Despite my desperate wish for my life to be normal in this town so I could focus on the dance and a cool dress …

Something just wasn't right.

CHAPTER 7

A Mysterious Discovery

AFTER SCHOOL THE next day, I waited for Jasper by my locker so we could go together to see our friends Alice and Lucinda. They were the magic experts in town, and they'd be able to give me some advice. I fidgeted while Mia and Amarjeet kept rehashing the dance lessons in every detail. The problem was none of us liked the lessons. They weren't helping us build team spirit. Instead, most of the guys resented the whole dancing idea as getting in the way of soccer, and most of the girls saw the lessons as getting in the way of the guys wanting to go to the Valentine's dance. I guess that united us somewhat – but probably not in the way Ms. Dreeble and Mr. Morrows hoped.

As for my teachers, I was more than a little puzzled by the way Ms. Dreeble and Mr. Morrows danced away each lesson, hardly noticing us at all. Also, Mr. Morrows looked so different after shaving off his mustache. What was up with that?

"The boys are in bad moods the whole time during our dance class. So how are you supposed to let a boy know you like him anyway?" complained Amarjeet. She banged her locker shut in frustration. At the beginning of the year, she'd liked Jasper, but lately all she talked about was Rabinder. Then Amarjeet turned to me and said, "It's not like *I'm* invited to the popular kids' table like *some people* so I could chat with Rabinder at lunch."

"But …" I stammered. "I was just brainstorming about the decorations with everyone at that table."

Amarjeet rolled her eyes. "Yeah, right. I overheard all the girls talk about the great dresses they were going to wear. Not everyone can get their parents to spend a fortune on clothes, you know? I was surprised to hear you going along with it all."

My face burned. What was wrong with wanting something fancier than an outfit that would make me look like a Christmas ornament?

"Who cares?" Mia sighed. "I don't think Mitch would notice me if I wore a gorgeous dress or a potato sack. He probably wouldn't notice me if I grabbed him by the shoulders and shouted it in his face. He's so busy complaining about every dance step when he's my partner." Mia frowned in disgust.

"If you like someone and want them to go to the dance with you, just ask them!" I exploded with impatience. If only *I* could worry about small things instead of a creepiness I couldn't shake, and how it might be tied to a sister whose magic had the tendency to spin out of control. Jasper joined us, and for some reason, gave me a dark look.

"Think about it, Cat," said Mia. "What fun would it be getting turned down by someone who doesn't know you exist."

I guess I hadn't looked at it that way. Maybe because I knew there was no hope that the boy I might be interested in would ask me to any dance. Zach would definitely take Emily if he showed up at all. "Well … we could all just go together and be dazzling and let other boys sweep us off our feet," I joked.

Mia grabbed her backpack and turned to Amarjeet. "Guess it all works out fine when you can afford clothes so expensive they're just like on T.V." Then Mia gently shook her head at me saying softly, "Maybe you've forgotten that for the rest of us, life's a little more complicated." Then she and Amarjeet left me standing with Jasper.

It's not like I was pretending I had loads of designer clothes, or that I wanted the dress because it was expensive. I was going to have to work hard to get it. "Let's go," I said to Jasper. I wished my friends were happier about the dance. My vision of having loads of fun with everyone was starting to evaporate. If only I could think of a way to get *everyone* on board.

As Jasper and I walked to the Greystones' house, I filled him in on Sookie's gardening abilities, which raised his eyebrows.

We climbed up the wrap-around porch of the Greystones' old-fashioned house, and once more I banged on the lion-head brass knocker – at least this doorknocker didn't send chills up my arm.

Alice opened the door and invited us in with a smile. "Are you here looking for odd jobs, Cat? Lucinda and I saw your poster on the Emporium window and we've been making a list. We were going to call you this week. If you want, you could start right now. We were hoping you'd help us clear boxes from the garage."

If only that was why I was here. A regular life – that's all I wanted. "Actually I'm a little worried about Sookie.

She's got a new hobby – gardening."

"Why would that worry you, Cat? Gardening's my favorite hobby," said Lucinda who came in from the kitchen. She was in a green gardening smock and held a pair of clippers. "I'm no use at cooking," she winced. "But I love spending time in my garden."

"But do your potted plants grow a foot in two days? In February?" I asked. A look of alarm crossed Alice's face, but Lucinda grew thoughtful.

"Fairy is nature at its wildest and most potent," mused Lucinda. "Sookie has visited Fairy twice now, and magic is in her blood. Maybe this would be a safe way for her to practice."

"But I don't want my sister doing magic at all," I said as worry swept over me yet again. I stared at the pattern of the Oriental rug for a second, embarrassed as I said, "I just want a normal sister."

Jasper snickered. "Well, that will never be Sookie. She wasn't exactly normal before we had trouble with Grim Hill fairies."

"Also," said Lucinda, "asking your sister to keep her magic bottled up inside her is like asking her not to speak. And you know how she loves her words. This might work out, Cat. Letting her practice with her plants might be a good way to channel some of her – well – peculiar energies."

Once Alice and Lucinda had managed to calm my fears about Sookie, we spent the better part of the evening lugging boxes out of the garage. I was carrying an old-fashioned cookie tin when I tripped over an ancient bicycle that Jasper had dragged out. The tin fell from my arms, spilling faded cards of paper lace and delicate ribbon.

"Woops, I'm really sorry." I began gathering up the cards.

"It's all right, dear." Lucinda stooped and picked up a beautiful heart-shaped card. "You've kept my valentines all these years," she said to her sister in surprise.

Alice Greystone smiled sadly. "I never actually looked inside the tin. I don't know what compelled me to hang onto it all those years during our dark times." That's how Alice referred to the seventy years she'd lived without her sister, who had been stolen by the fairies and was not released until she was a very old lady.

"What were years to you only seems like months to me," Lucinda said as her sad expression deepened the wrinkles in her face. Then she smiled and said, "For example, these cards only feel months old to me." Lucinda and Alice finished gathering the cards and placed them in the tin that I was holding.

"Oh," gasped Alice. "Even *I* remember this card." She held up a large valentine – the most spectacular card of all – a crimson foil heart that was still shiny after all these years. It glowed in the faint garage light.

"It's beautiful," I said.

"He would have chosen only the very best for Lucinda," Alice said. She flipped over the card and written in bold block letters was: *Valentine, be forever mine. Love, Gordie.*

"Remember how Gordie used to torment you?" Alice asked Lucinda. "How he'd dip your braids in the inkwell on his desk, or the time he carved both your names in the biggest oak tree at the church picnic and showed everyone! You were mortified." Alice shook her head. "He'd ride by our house every day on his bicycle hoping to catch a glimpse of you. He was madly in love with you from the second grade right on through to the seventh grade. He even wanted to take you to your first high school dance."

"Ah, the dance!" Lucinda exclaimed. "Oh, our gymnasium looked lovely – I was on the decorating committee and we'd hung silver and crimson foil hearts everywhere, and festooned the ceiling in white and red crepe paper. We'd even hung glowing Japanese silk lanterns. It seemed … magical."

My heart sped up. "Wow, I found decorations just like that in the art storage room at school. The foil hearts, the crepe paper, and the silk lanterns. They couldn't possibly be the same ones, could they?"

"Maybe not if it were only hearts and streamers," said Jasper. "But Japanese lanterns?"

More quietly Lucinda said, "If they are the *same* decorations from my dance, that would make them around seventy years old."

I was trying to remember what else I'd found there too, but then Alice slumped down on her red velvet wingback chair and didn't appear happy.

"Seventy years is a bad number in fairy dealings," Alice said in alarm.

As if the wind had snuffed out a candle, the room got a little darker.

CHAPTER 8

Lost Love

AROUND HALLOWEEN I'D managed to read a few pages from a grimoire – a book of instruction for fairy students. The book said that every seventy years the fairies had to take humans as a tithe to keep a hold in the human realm. "Do you think the two dances are connected to ..." I gulped, "the fairies in Grim Hill?"

"No," Lucinda said with authority. She began pacing by her fireplace, its mantel decked with pictures of the two elderly sisters making the most of the time they had together. "Grim Hill is sealed up tight. I feel it in my bones."

I let myself relax a bit.

"But ..."

The back of my neck tingled and then knotted up.

"But what?" Jasper balled his hand in a fist, and Alice sat straight in her chair.

Lucinda said, "There was something about Valentine's ... the February before I was locked away with the fairies ... something about that dance ..." It was Lucinda's turn to slump down on the matching velvet couch. She rubbed her forehead. "Sorry – it's all a foggy."

Alice grew thoughtful as she turned the foil card over and back again. "Whatever happened to Gordie?" she asked softly.

A tear welled in Lucinda's eye. Would I ever end up getting so nostalgic over a pest like Clive? I seriously doubted it. He gave me a hard time every chance he got. Jasper said we were too much alike. Mom said maybe it was Clive's way of getting my attention. I thought we just didn't like each other much.

For a long while Lucinda stayed quiet and then she began to tell a story – as much to herself as to us. She put the foil heart back down in the pile of cards, and as she began to speak, her voice seemed to be coming from a far-away place:

"In the second grade I was a lonely little girl with a terrible temper," Lucinda said. *"No one would be my friend. There was a boy in my class who always fidgeted in his desk and had broken crayons and messy handwriting. He was forever sent to stand in the cloakroom for speaking out of turn or telling tall tales."*

He sounded a bit like Sookie's friend Skeeter if you asked me.

"No one would play with him at recess because he was always getting in trouble at school. The other children were wary of him and they thought he was unpredictable. But when it was May Day, all the boys had to choose partners to dance with around the Maypole. I knew no boy in my class would pick me." Then Lucinda fell silent again.

That would feel awful, and I began to worry how that might happen to me at the dance if I kept stomping on people's feet. Suddenly I wondered if having someone like Clive ask me to dance was better than nobody asking me at all. Then I thought probably not.

Lucinda began her story once more. *"Nobody would*

pick me except that boy Gordie. He walked straight up to me and asked me to be his partner for the May Day dance. And even though he was a wild boy, he was handsome with brown curly hair and the biggest green eyes, and some of the girls in my class sent jealous glances my way. He was bold, but he knew enough not to leave me out. He understood what it felt like to be excluded."

"But I saw a lot of valentines in your tin. You must have gotten more popular," I reasoned.

"Oh I did," said Lucinda now seeming to grow more aware of her surroundings. "By eighth grade I was the belle of the class with many friends vying for my attention."

"And Gordie?" I asked. "Did he get more popular too?"

"Not at all." Lucinda's face darkened, and she pulled a plain cardboard valentine from the table with a hastily scribbled "Happy Valentine's" and held it up. "This card is not very special – not like the one Gordie labored so hard over. But when I received Roger's card, how thrilled it made me feel. He was the most popular boy in my grade and his paying attention to me meant I had to be the most popular girl."

That would be cool, I thought, remembering how eagerly I'd wanted the same thing back in the fall when I'd started school. But it would be awkward if some other person had asked you to the dance, and you had to turn them down to go with a person in your own crowd. Maybe I understood Mia and Amarjeet and their anger a little better.

"Gordie was never afraid of anything," said Lucinda.

68

"He was so brazen." And then Lucinda got that far-off sound in her voice again.

"Mother had sewn me a blue taffeta dress for the dance with bell sleeves. That was cutting-edge fashion back then. Alice was so envious I had to hide the dress in my closet or I'd come home from school and find her flouncing around in it."

Alice laughed and her eyes glowed. I could tell the memory warmed her. Also, that's exactly what Sookie would do.

Then Lucinda frowned and grew pale. *"Bold as brass, a few days before the dance, Gordie marched up to me and right in front of everyone said, 'Cindy, I want you to go to the dance with me'."*

"That would be … awkward," Jasper said as he sat down beside Lucinda on the red couch. "What did you do?" He had a curious tone to his voice – as if it mattered deeply what Lucinda had done.

"I stood there feeling mortified. I wish I could say I was trying to spare Gordie's feelings when he'd asked me to the dance – he had a genuine affection for me," began Lucinda. *"But the truth was that I was completely selfish. I knew I'd have to turn him down so that Roger would be assured I'd go to the dance with him. I walked up to Gordie right in front of Roger and in my cruelest voice said that I wouldn't go with him if he was the last boy on Earth. I was so unkind."* Lucinda blinked back tears.

"But my friend Ann had been standing beside me at that moment. She jumped in and also said in front of everyone, in an even louder voice, that I was 'cuckoo,' or as you young people say nowadays, 'nuts'…"

I didn't interrupt her to mention we would just

say "crazy."

"Ann said how any girl would be happy to go to the dance with Gordie – and would he please go with her."

"So did he end up going with Ann?" I asked as I thought, *Please tell me things turned out all right.*

Lucinda shook her head, and at first I thought it was because my voice had snapped her back to the here and now. But instead she clutched Gordie's valentine, and I couldn't help notice how it quivered in her trembling hands.

"You know," Lucinda said, "I remember the beginning of the dance – how much fun it was – but the rest is a fog. My time gets all mixed up lately."

Lucinda was very old and I worried how pale she'd become – her skin was almost translucent and her clear crystal eyes had somehow faded since the last time I'd seen her. Lucinda wrung her hands together. "I just don't remember whom I went with, or if Gordie came at all. But I think that at the time it was all just typical teen trouble, Cat, not fairy trouble …"

So the dance went off fine. Lucinda and her classmates had enjoyed themselves. If the dance had gone wrong, would the boxes of decorations still be sitting on our art shelf? Darkmont wasn't exactly the type of school that updated equipment regularly. There was no budget to discard stuff that was still in good shape.

The rest of the evening, Jasper and I carried boxes out of the Greystones' garage. When we'd finished, Alice came out and dug through her leather handbag. "How much do we owe you two for cleaning the garage?"

"Nothing," Jasper and I both said in surprise.

"Please, I insist." Alice placed twenty dollars each in Jasper's and my hands.

"Thank you, but ..." I said, feeling funny taking their money. They were our friends. It didn't seem right.

"We shouldn't ..." Jasper handed his money back, but Alice refused to take it.

"Well ... thank you. This is great because I'm trying to earn enough money to buy a dress for our Valentine's dance." I folded the money in my pocket.

"You buy a new dress and have fun," said Lucinda as she stepped out on the porch. She seemed shaky, and she'd wrapped herself in a heavy shawl.

As Jasper and I got ready to leave, Alice whispered to me, "Enjoy your dance. Just be careful, Cat."

CHAPTER 9

Love's Dangerous Charm

ON FRIDAY, DANCE lessons reached a low point. The girls had thought the lessons would be their big opportunity to secure their partners for the Valentine's dance. But Mr. Morrows and Ms. Dreeble had us rotate to new partners with each new song. Mr. Morrows kept barking out, "Switch partners!" as he swept around the room with Ms. Dreeble in his arms. Was that a whiff of cologne I detected?

The guys didn't seem to mind all the partner changing. Currently Mitch and Zach were competing with each other on how hard they could spin their partners. When Mitch tossed Amanda high in the air and she let out a frightened cry, Mr. Morrows bellowed, "Enough, Mitch. That's your last warning. This is *ballroom* dancing, not *swing* dancing – no tossing."

"Ow. Stop watching everyone else and stomping on my foot," my current partner complained to me.

"Sorry," I said. I'd danced with four boys in the last half hour and stomped on all their feet. If I didn't get the hang of this fox-trotting and rumba-ing, no one would come near me at the dance. I tried concentrating, but just as I was getting into the rhythm and matching my slide steps, Ms. Dreeble announced, "Please change partners."

Clive grabbed my hand. "Do you think you can

manage a few basic steps without falling on your butt?"
he asked with a smirk on his face.

For someone who had lots of complaints when we
danced, I wondered why Clive chose me for his partner
every single time – no matter how I tried to dodge him.
Whatever. Using my *über*soccer-goal focus, I counted
steps and remembered which foot went first and I
followed his lead. Until, that is, Mr. Morrows switched the
song and we were now supposed to waltz. It's pretty hard
to waltz when you try to stay as far away from a boy as
possible, only lightly grazing your hand over his and not
putting your other hand on his shoulder. It's a logistical
problem really, because that way you can't anticipate
which direction the boy is going in and …

"Hey! You stepped on my foot on purpose," Clive
complained loudly.

"No I didn't."

"Cat, that paragraph I asked you to write – make it
a five-hundred-word report," Ms. Dreeble shouted over
her shoulder as Mr. Morrows sashayed her around the
dance floor.

"Now look what you did," I argued with Clive.

"It's your own fault," he said taking my hand firmly
and trying to propel me across the dance floor. "You heard
the teacher before: guys are supposed to be the leaders."

As if! And when Clive launched into the next step, I
snatched my hand away. He overshot his stride and
collided with Zach, who then collided with Jasper, who'd
finally managed to get Mia as his partner. Suddenly all
the guys thought it was hilarious to collide with each
other, and I had to leave the gym quickly before Ms.

Dreeble blamed me.

But others blamed me.

***

"Cat, it's hard enough to get the boys to pay attention to us on the dance floor without you starting a stupid chain reaction." Mia stepped in front of me as Emily, Amanda, and Lea were taping foil hearts all over the wall. We'd already begun decorating the gym with the Valentine's decorations, but we were planning to leave the lanterns until last, so some stupid boys wouldn't knock them all down with basketballs. Not that I was mentioning any names.

"The next time we were to change partners, I would have been with Mitch," Mia almost shouted. "But *no*, you don't cause any trouble when I get all the boring dancers. Just as I'm about to dance with the boy I like, you have to get into it with Clive, and we *all* get dismissed early from the lesson."

I was glad Jasper wasn't with us. That would have hurt his feelings. He wasn't boring. He was smart and brave, and well, lots of great things that Mia just didn't notice. And why don't my friends ever see Clive's role in all this? At least Jasper didn't constantly pester Mia to get her attention. Then Amarjeet lit into me.

"Rabinder was my partner for the first time since we began dance lessons," she complained. "And we only danced together for about thirty seconds, thanks to you."

I didn't like the angry scowls on my friends' faces. Then Amanda said, "It's not like the boys need any help hating this idea. I wonder if we'll get them on board for the dance – yes, Emily, even if you wear an awesome dress."

Emily gave her a cold stare.

All of a sudden I realized that relationships were like soccer, and that if you just sat around and waited for the ball to come to you, you'd never accomplish anything. You had to be strategic and plan ahead. Then I looked at Lea and got an idea – one of the best ones I ever had. "Maybe there's a way for us to charm those boys into going to the dance."

Both Mia and Amarjeet dropped their scowls, and Emily and Amanda turned their heads my way. They all said simultaneously, "How?" Now I had my friends' attention.

"Lea," I whispered, "what were those herbs you said that help you find your true love?"

Lea laughed. "Lavender, yarrow, and maybe twitch grass and catnip."

"Love charms," I stalled as I said with authority to everyone. "I might be able to come up with love charms for the girls."

"Say again?" asked Amarjeet.

"Well," I said, now remembering more about what Lea had told me about some of the plants in Sookie's garden. "Some herbs are known for their romantic qualities. If you slip yarrow under a pillow, you will find out about your true love."

"Sweet," said Mia.

"That doesn't sound practical," Amarjeet frowned. "How exactly are you going to sneak a love charm under someone's pillow?"

"Maybe you don't have to do that to make a charm work," I began. Lea smiled reassuringly, prompting me to say, "I'll figure out a way." I actually had no idea.

"I guess it can't hurt. We obviously need all the help we can get," said Amarjeet.

The three other girls nodded. "Count us in."

Even Emily said, "Yeah, Zach won't go to the dance if his friends won't go."

Soon we were swarmed with other girls all wanting to get in on my plan. I'd gained the favor of practically every girl at dance class.

I only hoped I could deliver.

CHAPTER 10

Digging up Trouble

SATURDAY EVENING I should have been excited going over to Lea's house. Digging the garden would give me more money to buy my dress, and I really wanted to hang out with Lea. But there was a clunky, sick feeling in my stomach. I hoped I wasn't getting a flu. Sookie, however, danced on our porch like a top spinning out of control.

"How can you even grow plants in February?" shouted Skeeter over our back gate. He and Jasper had arrived. "Can I help?" In a shot, Skeeter was on the patio, and in moments, dirt was flying everywhere. A pot got knocked over despite Sookie's frantic directions.

"Where's Clive?" I asked. Trust him to back out at the last minute. And I'd promised Bea he'd be there.

"He's meeting us at the witch's house," piped Skeeter.

"I told you about a hundred times. It is *not* a witch's house," explained Sookie. "You shouldn't be judgmental."

"*Judge* what? Is so! I saw one in the backyard – an evil, ugly witch." Skeeter used his hands to tug his face into an ugly grimace.

"Well you have a pretty weird idea of what ugly is," I said, thinking about how attractive Lea and her aunt were. "You'll see."

77

Skeeter shook his head doubtfully, but he didn't seem any less enthusiastic about going over there. I hoped he wouldn't say anything awful. I'd worked out with Mom that Jasper and I would leave first while Sookie and Skeeter played for a while. That would give us time to hang out with Lea before the pests arrived. As we were leaving, I found Mom in the sewing room pinning patterns and stitching seams.

"Bye, Mom. Jasper and I are off to Lea's."

Mom glanced up from my outfit she was sewing and said, "Fine, see you later," and then she turned back to her sewing machine.

I felt I should say I was saving for a dress and she didn't have to waste her time, but what if I didn't make enough money? Except that wasn't it, I told myself. I knew she'd be disappointed, and I didn't want to tell her I didn't really like the skirt and blouse she was making me. So instead I said, "Skeeter's already in the backyard with Sookie."

Mom looked up at me, dropped her material, and rushed outside. Skeeter was an okay kid, but things just had a way of breaking when he played nearby.

As Jasper and I walked up the path to Lea's, it was as if all the gathering dark settled thickly around her house. The shadow of Grim Hill stretched right through her yard. Another easterly wind began blowing, banging shudders and creaking the railing as Jasper and I climbed the staircase.

"Wow," said Jasper. "This house is a lot creepier in the evening."

Strange how it could look so deserted on the outside,

but be so cozy on the inside. I lifted the doorknocker and crashed it against the door. We waited a while before the bolt rattled back and the door opened.

"Cat, Jasper, hi!" Lea wore an amazing green tunic with skinny jeans and emerald sheepskin boots. Again I smoothed out my plain jeans and faded brown sweater, and wiped my black sneakers on the mat. I wished I'd dressed better – even for digging up dirt.

Lea's hair glowed in the dim hall light like crimson stained glass, and it was pulled back revealing a sharp widow's peak that gave her face a heart shape. My dad used to call me his "October girl" because of my cat-green eyes, and he called Sookie his "sunshine girl" because of her blond hair. I wondered if Lea's dad called her his "Valentine girl" because of the shape of her face. And then I wondered about her mom. Did Lea even have parents? She never mentioned them.

Right away Lea whisked us up to her room, and Jasper did a double-take of all her books. Even he was impressed, and in no time Lea had loaned him a book of poems, which he tucked in his bag.

"Girls like poetry, right?" he asked us. I guessed so, but Lea assured him most girls did.

That was the neat thing about Lea, she had it all: looks, coolness, and loads of clothes, books, and jewelry, but it was as if it all meant little to her. I suspected you could ask for anything of hers, and she'd give it to you. Even though she'd been invited into Darkmont's coolest inner circle, she only seemed to join those kids if I was there. She didn't hang out with anyone else after school. I got the feeling she was a bit of a loner, actually.

I wondered if she'd had many friends in her old town – if she'd been as popular. I was so curious, I asked, "So what town did you live in before? Do you keep in touch with your old friends?"

Lea hung her head and mumbled something in a strange whispery voice she got when she spoke softly. It almost sounded like rustling paper caught in the wind. Then a terrible racket broke out downstairs. Someone was mercilessly hammering the doorknocker. Jasper and I looked at each other and said, "Clive's here." I hoped Lea appreciated me sacrificing our time together so her aunt could have another helper.

When we opened the door, it amused me to see Clive's eyes wide with nervousness. So he didn't appreciate waiting out there on the porch in the dark. He always tried to make it seem as if he was so brave … actually, he sort of was, but that didn't mean it should always go to his head. As soon as he saw me, he smirked. As Lea ushered him inside, Mom dropped off Sookie and Skeeter and they rushed up the steps.

As they came in, Skeeter whispered something in Sookie's ear, and I overheard, "Let's look for the witch." My face burned, but when I glanced at Lea, she seemed not to have heard. Sookie simply shook her head.

"Ah, my gardeners have arrived." Aunt Bea came out from the back of the house dressed in a peculiar gardening outfit. A long silky grey dress that swirled around her bare feet.

Skeeter for once had nothing to say. We went out back and all grabbed shovels from the garden shed.

"What's in there?" asked Skeeter.

At the end of the backyard, a whole section of the garden next to the graveyard had been closed in – the part of the garden that I'd seen dug up before. A tall fence had been built since I'd last been here, and amazingly, a tangle of thorny vines had already sprung up and covered the fence. That was fast. Sookie-fast. I grew wary. Skeeter ran over to the gate and tugged.

"It's locked," he complained.

"That is where I keep my most delicate flowers," said Bea. "I close it off to keep it safe from pests."

For a second, I thought Lea's aunt was talking about Skeeter, but then she smiled and said in a voice that sounded a bit chilling, "I cannot abide cats digging in my special garden."

We got right to work. I lifted a garden pick and slammed it hard into the ground over and over again. Pretty soon a blister boiled on my hands, and Lea kindly ran off to fetch me a pair of thick gardening gloves. Jasper and Clive dug into the ground with their shovels and turned up dense clods of grass.

Sookie waltzed around in a ridiculous gardening outfit: a gigantic yellow straw hat, rubber boots, and an apron with pockets stuffed with miniature gardening tools. Sookie hovered by Lea's aunt and helped her dig out potted plants all the while asking her endless questions about herbs.

"Go play with Sookie," I urged Skeeter. He could be pretty obedient when he wanted to be. He dropped his shovel and ran toward her.

Lea carried out plant trays from the shed and from a broken-down greenhouse, and piled them by the garden.

I noticed how every time she walked our way, Jasper and Clive stopped digging, leaned on their shovels, and got goofy smiles on their faces. It was hard work and their behavior slowed us down even more.

Next, Skeeter tried sneaking a peek at the closed garden. When he tried crawling under the gate, Lea's aunt moved quickly toward him, and for some reason, my heart sped up.

"You need a special job," was all she said to Skeeter. "Why don't you come into the shed with me? I've got something I think you'll like."

When Skeeter came out, he carried a drum. You could hold the drum in your hand like a large tambourine and bang it with both ends of a stick.

"What kind of a drum is that?" I asked Bea.

"It's Irish," Bea said. "Skeeter, why don't you beat out a rhythm for us all to keep pace. It will make the work go faster."

With enthusiasm, Skeeter started banging away. Oddly enough, it was as if my heart began to match each beat. When Skeeter quickened the pace, so did I. Before we knew it, the garden was ready for planting. Skeeter kept up the drumming, and in a short time all of Bea's plants were tucked into the soil. All except for about a dozen plants that Bea had given to Sookie to bring home.

Then as bold as could be, Skeeter asked, "If you gave Sookie some plants, can I keep the drum?"

My face flushed and then I thought, *Hey, he's not my brother*. I looked at Clive. He simply shrugged his shoulders.

Bea seemed unfazed. She smiled at Skeeter and said,

"Certainly." Then she came over and paid Clive, Jasper, and me fifty dollars each!

"Wow, thanks," said Clive pocketing his money. Jasper thanked her profusely. So did I.

I calculated my money in my head. With the twenty dollars from the Greystones', plus this cash, plus the hundred I'd make with Mr. Keating – "Hey, I'm only ten dollars short of affording the dress I want to buy at Esmeralda's," I blurted.

"Far be it for me to stand in the way of your dress," said Bea, and she placed ten more dollars in my hand. "Maybe you could come by tomorrow and help clean up. It's getting late for that now."

"Really? That's fantastic," I said, thrilled. "Thank you."

"That stupid dance," said Clive. "You should be spending time working on your soccer plays. You're just as distracted as the rest of the girls."

"Who put you in charge?" I asked, not a bit embarrassed to be arguing in front of Lea and her aunt.

That is, until Sookie said with a humph, "It's not so fun getting bossed around, is it, Cat?"

Ignoring Sookie, I suddenly wished that Lea could come to the dance too. Everything was falling into place – me getting the dress, and my friends looking forward to Valentine's again. "Not everyone thinks the dance is stupid," I said glaring at Clive. "Loads of kids will be going to the dance next Friday – practically everyone in our grade. Maybe even Lea?"

I hadn't exactly asked if Lea could go – I only put it out there. But one look at Lea's face made me regret it. She went pure white, which wasn't easy as her skin was already fair.

"I'm afraid Lea will be busy that night," said Bea.

"Why? What are you doing Friday night?" I asked Lea as we were leaving. But Bea was right beside us, and before Lea could answer, her aunt sent her into the kitchen to put on the kettle. Lea said goodbye to us and then went inside.

"Your friend Lea's cool," Clive said as we walked through the side yard to get to the gate. Even though I was with Sookie, Jasper, Clive, and Skeeter, I got the oddest feeling.

I didn't believe in ghosts, even though I'd thought I'd seen a ghost once. That time I'd been wrong. Still, I thought I could tell when I was having a brush with the supernatural. A cold chill settled over my skin as I passed the creepy tangled vines that grew along the graveyard, and something made the hair stand up on the back of my arms and neck as if I'd brushed through a cobweb. I could feel the stickiness cling to me.

Everyone chatted happily as we left the front gate and headed home.

Why couldn't I relax?

CHAPTER 11

A Deadly Mix

THAT NIGHT I tossed and turned and kept my lamp on all night – the shrill wail of the easterly wind was getting to me. Sunday morning I was still quite groggy, so as I was snipping lavender and yarrow from Sookie's potted plants – or what I'd now call Sookie's jungle – it took a minute for me to process what Sookie was yammering on about.

"You don't have all the ingredients," Sookie almost shouted.

At first I was confused and thought she'd been talking about the pancakes Mom was making. "Huh?" I asked.

"For the love charms you're assembling," Sookie said, getting impatient. "Those ingredients will never work. Not if you want to conjure a good spell."

"What was that?" Mom called from the kitchen as she flipped pancakes.

"Oh nothing," Sookie said in her most innocent voice that still fooled Mom – sometimes.

"I'm not casting a spell," I said as I glared at my sister. "And neither are you. This is simply a little bit of fun – I'm only giving the girls a little push in choosing a partner for the dance instead of always complaining about it and blaming me. I don't care if these charms actually work."

"That doesn't sound like the real reason," Sookie frowned as her face clouded with doubt.

"I want to get along better with my friends. They seem to think I'm ... well, they just don't get me, and this seems to make them happy."

"I want your friends to like you, Cat. Can I at least help a little?" Sookie proceeded to bug me all through breakfast.

"Fine," I said. "You can help me sew the bags for the charms." I was no good with a needle and thread anyway, and this would keep my sister from driving me crazy.

Later that afternoon, I used the mortar and pestle from my old chemistry set to crush the buds of sweet-smelling lavender. Then I sprinkled the crumbled petals into Mom's big mixing bowl. I stifled a sneeze – between the dust in the attic and the flowers and seeds, my allergies were acting up. Reaching over to the pile of herbs on the table, I grabbed the catnip and mashed it up. "Here's to the power of love."

Sookie scowled as she watched me. "Cat, why do girls want boys to go crazy over them?"

"You'll understand in a few years," I assured her. I sliced the stem of yarrow and remembered how Lea had said if I slept with it under my pillow, I'd see the initials of my true love. Staring at the stem, I thought suddenly, *What if there were no initials there for me, or if there were initials of someone I didn't like*. Better not to know, I decided, crushing the stem and throwing it into the mixture.

Sookie sprinkled the crushed buds into red conjure bags. I really hoped Mom wouldn't miss her old red scarf.

Sookie had gotten a bit carried away and declared only red silk would do, and she'd cut it into squares and had sewn the squares up like pockets before I realized what she'd been up to.

"These charms will work better if the girls gather in a circle and stand under a February storm moon at midnight." Sookie took a red conjure bag and held it to her chest. "Then each girl has to hold the charm like this, choose the boy she likes, and say his name out loud." Then with a sly smile she said, "Then all of you must hang the conjure bag around that boy's neck."

"I don't think that's going to happen," I laughed. "Plus, how would we all ever get together at midnight?"

"You could invite your friends for a sleepover. That would be fun, and then they'd like you again."

"That's not a bad idea," I said, wondering if Mom would allow it. I could invite the popular girls and my old friends, and if everyone enjoyed themselves, I wouldn't feel pulled in all directions. I could make everyone happy.

"Are you sure you don't want to let me add some Spanish moss, which makes the charm potent, or some licorice root so the boys shouldn't even notice they're falling under your power?" Sookie asked.

The Spanish moss was the eerie-looking plant – all grey and kind of wormy. And I remembered Lea's half-joking warning about the licorice root. I shuddered. "No way."

"But if you mix the moss with mullein, you should be able to get the boys under your spell – at least that's what Auntie Bea advised."

"No way, Sookie, there will be no casting spells. This

is supposed to be for fun. And I thought I told you Bea wasn't your aunt."

"Mom said I could call her that," she said, but she didn't talk about Bea again. Instead she seemed deep in thought as she finished sewing up the conjure bags. I scooped up the love charms and tossed them in my backpack.

"Tuesday is a district professional day at school," said Sookie. "We all get a holiday, so why don't you ask Mom if you can have the sleepover tomorrow night? There's going to be a storm."

"How do you know?"

"I just do," Sookie said mysteriously. I wasn't sure I'd ever get used to my sister's strange abilities.

"Maybe," I said. I guess if I wanted a sleepover, that would be the only available way we could get together, activate the love charms, and pass them on to the boys in time for the dance.

Sookie and I went to Bea's house in the afternoon to clean up. No one was at home as I picked up gardening tools and rinsed them off under the outdoor tap. Even though I was getting an extra ten dollars, I was regretting coming back here. No one was at home, and the backyard was dark even in the chilly February afternoon. Sookie was right – a storm was brewing on the horizon and the wind picked up, scattering old leaves into tiny tornadoes.

I didn't see how Bea's garden could grow so well without light – unless ... unless Bea and Sookie had more in common than gardening. Maybe that was what unsettled me – some of Grim Hill magic seeped right into this soil, and all it took was a gardener with special abilities to unlock the magic.

"Aren't you going to give me some of the money?" Sookie interrupted my thoughts. "I'm your assistant."

"Assistants don't get paid – this is *my* part-time job. But I'll treat you to bubble tea later this week."

Sookie frowned, but she didn't complain.

At dinner when Mom was pulling macaroni casserole out of the oven, I prepared to ask her about the sleepover. First I washed my hands and began setting the table. After dinner when Sookie begged to watch T.V., I scooped up a sponge and began washing dishes, even though I preferred drying them.

"Well, aren't you helpful tonight." Mom smiled and folded her arms. "So, what do you want?"

I decided to come straight out with it. "Could I have a sleepover tomorrow night? Please, please Mom?" I begged. "All my friends want to stay over and try out different hairstyles."

"Ah," Mom said knowingly. "You're all getting ready for the Valentine's dance on Friday."

"Exactly," I said in all honesty.

"So this means quite a few girls?" Mom asked.

I tried a charming smile as it usually worked for Sookie. "Most of the soccer team."

Mom's eyes widened. "Well …"

I held my breath as I swirled the suds of the dishwater and scrubbed the casserole dish.

"Maybe," said Mom. "I guess they could bring sleeping bags, and you could camp out in the attic." Then Mom gave me a stern look. "As long as you promise lights-out by eleven-thirty, because I need my sleep. I'll have work in the morning. Staff and teachers don't get the day off."

"You won't hear a peep," I promised. I waited and time seemed to stretch with each tick of the red kitchen clock.

Finally Mom said, "Well, who am I to stand in the way of all your important preparations?"

I almost jumped in excitement. Even though Alice had told me to stay watchful, visiting the Greystones had taken a weight off my chest – I could enjoy the Valentine's dance, I could make peace with Mia and Amarjeet. Maybe even Lea could come to the sleepover.

"A sleepover!" Sookie stood in the doorway and squealed with glee. "I can't wait."

Great. I should have known. Sookie would insist on hanging out with us. So that's why she suggested the sleepover and sneaking out to cast charms under a storm moon. I'd been set up. Suddenly I was regretting letting my little sister in on my problems.

***

Monday morning before school, I went to Esmeralda's dress shop after I'd finished up at Mr. Keating's. The shop wasn't open yet, but Esmeralda spotted me staring in the window and she opened the shop door for me. The smell of rose petals drifted out. "Yes?" queried Esmeralda without inviting me inside.

I pulled one hundred dollars out of my wallet – Mom would freak if she knew I was carrying that much cash around – and handed it to Esmeralda. "I'll have enough money on Wednesday for the dress I like, just as soon as Mr. Keating pays me."

Esmeralda leaned out of her door and called out to Mr. Keating as he stood under his striped awning admiring his vegetables. "Yoo-hoo, Mr. Keating! My, don't you look robust today."

Huh? What about my dress? And Mr. Keating didn't look robust. He appeared, well, round.

"Would you care to join me for some coffee?" Esmeralda asked him.

Mr. Keating gave her a distracted wave and then went inside his shop.

Esmeralda pursed her lips in a disappointed frown, but at least she remembered I was standing there. "Yes, the dress, certainly. I'll put it aside for you immediately." And then she closed her shop door. I would have liked to see the dress against me again, but I shrugged my shoulders and hurried to school.

Later at school, a cold and absolute terror surged through me.

"Cat, I asked you where your report is." Ms. Dreeble moved toward my lab table and leaned over me, peering at my binder.

I'd completely forgotten about writing my biology report and turning it in this Monday morning! I'd been too busy mixing love potions and mailing e-vites to my sleepover on Facebook. The acceptances started rolling in right away, and I stayed up late reading them – everyone I'd invited had accepted! Except that now …

Ms. Dreeble stood beside my desk and waited. It's

hard coming up with a good excuse when fear races through your brain.

"Um ..." I sputtered. "Symbiotic and parasitic relationships are ..." *think, Cat, think*, "... fascinating. I ..."

Lea grimaced in sympathy. Finally I said, "I got carried away with the research."

"Oh really," said Ms. Dreeble in a way I could tell she didn't believe a word. "Do tell us a bit about that research, Cat."

Amanda stuck up her arm, ready to step in if I couldn't deliver. I could feel sweat beading under my pink scarf, so I loosened it up at the neck. "Symbiosis," I said as I glanced at Lea who gave me an encouraging nod, "is a mutually ... beneficial ... relationship in the plant and animal world." I finished quickly.

Ms. Dreeble looked a bit surprised. "So that means what, Cat?" Was that enthusiasm in her voice? Amanda waved her arm.

"That plants and animals help each other," I said. "But it's the opposite in a parasitic relationship. In that case, one animal or plant is going to end up sick or even dead."

Whew. Ms. Dreeble actually smiled. Amanda dropped her arm, and I stopped sweating. Lea clapped her hands.

"Well, run with it, Cat." Ms. Dreeble nodded enthusiastically, maybe more to herself than to me. "Turn this research into a report, and I will give you bonus marks."

"Report?" I squeaked. "How long is a report?"

Ms. Dreeble tossed back her hair – were those new blond highlights? They shone even in the drab light of the classroom. "Well," she said, "If you've been researching it all weekend, I'm thinking you'll have enough information for the report to be about five pages long. You can have until next Monday."

Five pages! My doom was sealed. The bell rang and I threw my binder in my backpack.

I shook my head wondering how I'd managed to get myself an even bigger homework assignment with Ms. Dreeble, when Mia said laughingly, "Either you're going to end up a top science student or you'll end up with detentions your entire high school life." She shook her head. "I can't decide which."

"Sorry," said Lea.

At least Lea seemed to care about how Ms. Dreeble was always on my case. She didn't think it was all so funny. I hadn't sent an e-vite to Lea last night because she didn't have internet yet, but now I asked, "Can you come to my sleepover?"

Delight spread over her face as she tucked a strand of auburn hair behind her ear. "You're inviting me?"

Why would she seem so surprised? She really must have moved around a lot because I'd imagine she'd be the most popular girl in any neighborhood. Besides, I suddenly realized, despite the fact that everyone else had accepted, I hoped she'd come to my sleepover most of all. "So you'll be allowed?"

A shadow crossed her eyes. "Maybe I can come later ... for a while," she said. "I hope."

"Sure," I said. "Whatever time works for you."

Lea's aunt always seemed super nice. Even though she wasn't allowing Lea to go to the dance, I didn't see why she wouldn't be allowed to stay the whole time at my sleepover.

I just didn't get it.

But something about Lea's expression stopped me from pressing her further.

CHAPTER 12

A Storm Brews

AFTER SCHOOL, THE dance lessons started going better. I was able to relax and enjoy myself, but then I got distracted. Slide, back-step, slide … I couldn't wait for the sleepover … slide, back-step, slide … it would be a blast … turn and …

"Ouch. Watch it, Cat." Yet another boy looked over his shoulder, hoping to switch to a better dancer.

If only I could focus and remember to step back first with my right foot so I could twirl and sashay without a misstep. Not that Ms. Dreeble or Mr. Morrows noticed – they were too busy practicing the dance steps with each other. They got so caught up in waltzing around the gloomy gym as if they were dance stars, they forgot to demonstrate the new steps to us – not that I cared – which, I began to decide, was my problem with dancing. I just wasn't that interested. I liked fast dancing and bouncing around the gym a whole lot better. But no matter how many guys seemed reluctant to be my partner, somehow Clive ended up dancing with me again.

"Cat, your dancing really isn't so great for a – "

"Girl?" I said ready to step on his toes.

He shrugged his shoulders. "I was going to say for such a good soccer player. It's not like you can't do great footwork."

Well ... I loved soccer ...

"I was wondering if ..."Clive paused, and the slide-step of the other students and the tinny music on the dance CD drowned out other sounds. "Um ... although I wasn't exactly excited about this dance ..." Clive stumbled a bit, which wasn't his usual style.

Clive was – what had Lucinda called it? "Bold as brass." As if tiny needles jabbed my skin, I wondered what was up with him.

"Well," Clive began again. "Mr. Morrows offered our band a job playing at the dance; it seems there was enough money left over from the Christmas show – and well, jobs are hard to come by in this town ..."

I knew that. What was his point?

"Anyhow, you know my brother's in the band and ... um, you should see, ever since Skeeter got that drum from Lea's aunt, he can't stop playing it. He's way better than our band's last drummer."

"Right ..." What. Was. Clive. Getting. At.

"So, I, like, thought because Sookie is Skeeter's friend ... and I'm already going to be with him, and I'll have to stick around to take down the equipment, maybe if your mom brought Skeeter home, we could like ..."

Just then, Amanda swooped by with her dance partner, and she broke away and grabbed my arm. She dragged me off the dance floor leaving her partner and Clive standing there. Clive scowled.

"Are those love charms going to be ready soon?" Amanda asked. "The dance is only a few days away and we've got to get the guys on board."

"Sure, no problem – they're good to go. We'll be, um,

activating them at midnight at my sleepover."

"Awesome," said Amanda looking impressed.

Then Ms. Dreeble and Mr. Morrows dismissed us from the dance lesson. I got caught up in the mad rush and was pushed out the gym. I couldn't help notice Clive glaring at me. For some reason, it was almost a relief to see him back to his old self.

Outside, the wind was whipping around quite forcefully as Jasper and I made our way home. "I've been working on some poems," Jasper said. "I'm just not sure if they're ... um ... romantic."

"What?" I said in a rush as we stood in front of Esmeralda's dress shop. I stared at my dress. Esmeralda had hung it on the hold rack next to the window and had wrapped it in plastic. It looked like a gorgeous butterfly ready to escape its cocoon. I couldn't help thinking that wearing that dress might have the same effect on me. And Wednesday, that dress would be mine.

"Cat," Jasper said exasperated.

"Sorry," I said pulling myself away from the shop window. "It seems to me Lea is a better authority on poetry," I said in a distracted tone.

Maybe I hadn't sounded very interested in Jasper's poems because he said dismissively, "You're right, I should ask Lea." Then he hesitated before he asked, "Has anyone asked you to the dance?"

"Huh," I snorted. "Most boys can't stand being my partner for ten minutes during our dance lessons." Except for Clive. Wait a minute – even though he did nothing but complain, he always chose me as his dance partner. And exactly what had he been trying to ask me during the lesson? I looked at Jasper in alarm. Did he know something I didn't?

"Well," I said, "if some boy, say, someone such as Clive, thinks for a minute that I'd want to be his dance partner, that's his mistake."

"Just so you know," Jasper said with a tinge of bitterness, "it wouldn't exactly be cool asking a girl to a dance and have her turn you down."

Jasper was caught in a bad situation. He really wanted to ask Mia to the dance, but he knew she liked Mitch, even though Mitch didn't seem to be the least bit interested in her. I felt a little guilty helping Mia with a love charm for Mitch. Jasper was a good friend and I should really be helping him with a love charm for Mia, but then I shook it off. I couldn't help everybody, and it was just for fun anyway.

***

Mom was being cool about the sleepover, thank goodness. Ever since we had moved, it almost seemed as if she also wanted me to gain back my popularity. She even splurged and bought me an awesome new set of pj's – red silk shorts and a matching T printed with white hearts. Of course she had to get Sookie a matching nightgown. "They were on sale," Mom said, happy we liked them.

I hurried to get ready for my friends. Mom had bought frozen pizza bagels and miniature frozen taco rolls, so after dinner I began heating them in the oven. When they were done I left the oven on warm as I went upstairs to straighten up the attic.

There was a perfect storm moon that night. Even though black clouds scudded across the darkening sky, the moon peeked through.

"It's a gibbous moon," Sookie said looking out the window. "So that means the moon is waning. I'm worried that your charms won't be as potent."

Why was Sookie taking those stupid charms so seriously? I wished she'd just forget about them and go watch the kid DVDs Mom had rented to keep her out of my hair, but I knew there was as much chance of that as me head-butting a soccer ball across the field and straight into a goal. Actually, I had a much better chance at that. And then her interference got worse.

Sookie had kept a low-enough profile at the beginning of the sleepover as my friends arrived, and I'd even thought my sister had gone to bed around nine. But after Mom had turned in for the night and the clock struck half past eleven, Sookie burst into the attic, "I've got it, Cat! I've figured out how we can make the storm moon spell work better."

"Not a chance," I said. But I was out-voted ten to one by every other girl. Fifteen minutes later I simmered as my sister got all the attention. My sleepover wasn't exactly going as planned. I'd thought we'd all hang out and talk about girl stuff and laugh. But for one thing, Lea hadn't shown up. For another, as we huddled in our sleeping bags while the cold wind blew through the cracks of the drafty attic, we got the pleasure of being bossed around by a nine-year-old.

Sookie perched on a chair, making it seem as if she

towered over us beneath the sloped attic roof, as she lectured about how to cast the love spells. I couldn't shake how weird it felt having my kid sister take charge. I'd tried sending her back downstairs, but every single girl stayed rapt with attention as if Sookie was the most interesting teacher in the world. And Sookie loved every second of it.

As if Sookie had ordered sound effects, an eerie wail whined outside.

With dramatic gestures, she waved at the bone-colored moon and said in a spooky voice, "It's getting close to midnight, so we must gather near the graveyard."

Wait a minute, what? "We're only going to the back garden," I reminded everyone as I eyed my sister. But they all ignored me, and when Sookie grabbed the box of red conjure bags from under her chair, every girl took one and clutched it in her hand.

"I've decided the wind will whip graveyard dust up into the air, and that will make the spells work even better," Sookie said, waving her arm as if she was a potent wizard instead of a little girl dressed in a pink nightie printed with tiny hearts.

"Mom will ground me forever, and besides, that place is beyond creepy," I said, hoping everyone would listen to reason. But my friends didn't seem to care about me getting in trouble.

"Scaredy Cat," Sookie chuckled, as if she'd said the most hilarious thing in the world. "We don't have to go *into* the graveyard – just standing close to it should do."

"That should be okay," said Mia a bit nervously as she shrugged into her hoodie.

"I'm in," said Amarjeet. "As long as we don't have to disturb ... the dead ... in their sleep."

Emily raised her eyebrows. "You throw the most interesting parties, Cat," she said.

That sent a shiver through me. The last party I'd had ended in total disaster. But I couldn't think of a way to get out of this – especially not if I wanted to stay on everyone's good side.

My friends lined up to follow my sister who marched toward the stairs like a little general. Working with Sookie was like letting a genie out of a bottle.

"We'd better be quiet and not wake Mom," I said to no one in particular as I scooped up my own red conjure bag and scampered after everyone.

CHAPTER 13

Spells by Moonlight

AS WE APPROACHED the cemetery, I sort of thought it was a fitting place to be. After all, Mom would kill me if she found out that I was walking around at midnight with my kid sister and my friends. How did I get myself into this? It was wrong and I knew it. I could tell by how nervous Amarjeet and Emily were acting that they knew this was stupid as well. And I really didn't like graveyards.

When Sookie was little we'd visited a cemetery once so Dad could put flowers on our grandmother's grave. Sookie had stared at all the emerald green grass, the headstones, and the crosses sticking out of the ground and asked, "What's this place for, Daddy?"

"It's a park for dead people," our dad had said. I knew Dad was trying to find a gentle way to describe the place, and Sookie seemed satisfied by his answer. Maybe that's why she didn't seem even a little scared to be standing beside a graveyard right now. Maybe it was too late to back out, but we sure didn't have to stay long.

I wasn't the only one who couldn't stop shivering, and it wasn't only because I was freezing, wearing just my Valentine's pj's under my red wool coat.

"It's almost midnight," Sookie said in a hushed voice. "Gather in a circle and hold your conjure bags to your heart."

Amarjeet held up her red conjure bag, sniffed it suspiciously, and made a face. So did Mia. I held the silky material in front of my face and took a cautious sniff. Yuck – sure there were lavender scents, but there was also a musty smell that made me think of old bones or ancient mummies. Why? Those dried flowers shouldn't smell bad.

"Hurry," commanded Sookie. My friends crushed the bags to their chests. I also did exactly as my kid sister instructed, only unlike the other girls, I kept peering nervously over my shoulder. Some of the headstones were visible behind the graveyard gate, and it was as if that crumbling stone angel was staring straight at me.

"Do you really think this is a good idea?" I almost heard it say.

Behind the gate, bare tree branches twitched as if long witch fingers were saying, *"Come just a little closer."* Behind the graveyard, Grim Hill loomed like a hulking giant. Quickly I looked away and faced Lea's house, but it seemed as if all the clouds collected over that creepy place, and I couldn't shake the feeling we were being watched.

I thought about the soft eerie wailing I could hear from behind those thorny hedges. I could see them from where I was standing, and for a second I stared in amazement at how much the hedge had grown since the last time I was in Lea's backyard. Around her aunt's private garden, the vines were now at least seven feet tall and hung over the fence thick as snakes and dripped with huge nasty thorns.

"Now call out the name of your one true love,"

Sookie said with relish. Unlike me, she loved every moment of this.

So that I'd feel less jumpy, I imagined myself in that new dress with my shimmering scarf flowing behind me as I danced. I closed my eyes and pictured the boy I'd like to dance with. I'll admit it – even though I refused to be interested in a boy who couldn't care less about me – if wishes really came true, I'd like to go with a certain guy with blond hair, blue eyes, and a cute smile.

"Rabinder," Amarjeet whispered shyly.

"Louder," instructed Sookie.

Amarjeet swallowed and repeated, "Rabinder," in a ringing voice.

"Mitch!" Mia shouted enthusiastically.

Again, I checked over my shoulder wishing this was all over and acknowledging that maybe it *hadn't* been the smartest idea I'd ever had. Next it was Amanda's turn.

"Zach," she called out.

Huh?

Then it was Jennifer's turn. "Zach," she said glaring at Amanda.

"Me too," said Ashley. "I want to go to the dance with Zach."

The next girl also said, "Zach."

"Seriously!" Emily said in an irritated voice. "You all know I'm going with Zach."

So why did she have her own conjure bag, I thought, more than a little irritated myself. And all those other girls knew I'd probably be wishing for Zach too.

Sookie turned to me shaking her head. "Well, Cat, this is a conundrum."

It never occurred to me that a bunch of girls would call out the same boy's name – the boy who I'd wanted to take *me* to the dance. That's what I got for wishing for the most popular boy. By the time it came around to my turn, a total of five girls had wished for Zach to ask them to the dance. Emily and I were the last ones to call out a name, but she'd stomped off in a huff and stood up the street waiting for us. It seemed that having so many girls interested in Zach had made her a lot more interested in him herself.

As I decided there was little point in me saying anything, a horrible wail ripped through the air. We all screamed and jumped a foot off the ground before making a dash back to my house. I grabbed Sookie's hand, and as I ran, the cold wind whipped through my coat and slapped against my bare legs. Shivering, I urged my sister between chattering teeth, "Faster … hurry …"

We made it back to the yard, and when the last girl leaped inside the kitchen door, I heard someone call my name. Quickly I turned around and saw Lea standing in my yard. The moon was buried behind the clouds, and my friend looked like a silhouette against all the shadows.

"Lea?" I said in surprise. "Are you coming to the sleepover *now*?"

Lea hung her head. "Oh Cat," she said in a terribly mournful voice. "What have all of you done?"

"Mom's awake!" Sookie called to me in a panic. Torn between Lea's mysterious reply and Mom catching us, I stood rooted to the ground. But then Lea stepped back and disappeared into the shadows.

"Cat!" Sookie urged.

I ran and hurdled over one of Sookie's potted plants, brushing my bare legs against the feathery leaves as I hurried into the kitchen – and straight into Mom.

"Yes, Cat, exactly what on Earth are all of you girls up to?" Mom finished tying up her chenille housecoat tightly and put her hands on her hips.

Everyone began filing out of the kitchen and up to the attic, except for me and Sookie. "We were, um …" I squirmed under Mom's withering stare.

"What were you doing that would require your coats and shoes?" asked Mom – her voice rising in a seriously angry way. "I'm the responsible adult, and I trusted you. Now I find you girls roaming outdoors at midnight?" She stared coldly at my friends as they hurried up to the attic.

Mom looked really mad, really …

"Cat, I'm demanding to know what you were doing," Mom almost shouted. She never shouted. "I'm afraid there might not be a dance for you."

No – this couldn't be happening. I only needed one more paycheck and that dress was mine. And even if I wasn't able to cast a spell on Zach, surely some boy would dance with me. Now I wasn't even going to get a chance to find out.

"We were casting spells," Sookie smoothly said.

"Pardon?" asked Mom.

"We were just on the porch," Sookie said as I looked at her in surprise. That was a straight-out lie. Well, I guess we were on the porch when Mom caught us.

"If you stand under the moon and wish for your one true love," Sookie said in her usual over-dramatic way, "you can win that boy's heart."

Mom's face softened and then she laughed. "Next time you stand out on the porch and wish on the stars, please give me advanced notice." She shook her head and mumbled to herself, "At least you all put on coats. I don't want calls from angry parents that everyone's catching colds." Before she went upstairs, Mom did a double-take of the small jungle in our backyard. It was if she hadn't gotten around to noticing all the thriving plants. She shook her head in puzzlement before going back upstairs. I remembered that living next to a fairy hill tended to make adults not always notice the magic that seeped into our town.

"Sookie," I said. "You stretched the truth – that's the same as a lie."

My sister didn't seem to care. She beamed as she said, "Your friends like you a lot now, Cat. I heard them say this party was awesome."

They did? Well, that was good *and* we'd dodged trouble from Mom. I felt such relief when I crawled back into my sleeping bag and snuggled into its warmth; I started getting super drowsy. Just as I was about to drop off to sleep, my eyes flew open as I recalled what had happened before my run-in with Mom ...

Why was Lea so upset?

CHAPTER 14

A Dark Obsession

IT WAS TUESDAY afternoon by the time my friends left. Sookie and I headed to Lea's because I wanted to find out what had upset her the night before. Sookie came with me, but as she leaped up the steps, I dragged my feet. As stupid as it sounded, I was uneasy. If there was such a thing as haunted, it would be this house.

Ignoring the prickling sensation over my arms and scalp, I climbed the stairs to Lea's place. I clanged their creepy mad-dog doorknocker – but nobody was home.

"C'mon, Cat, I have things to do," complained Sookie.

"What do you have to do? You're only nine," I complained. "And besides, I thought you liked coming here."

"I'm very busy, you know," was all Sookie would say.

I hoped the fact that Lea and her aunt were out meant Lea was feeling better. I pulled a piece of paper out of my backpack, scribbled a note inviting Lea to come over later, and stuffed it in the mailbox.

As I came down the steps, I could hear creaks and groans from the backyard, and I wondered if maybe they were there. We walked around back, and I saw how Bea's garden had grown in a wild jungle-like way, just like Sookie's potted plants. Actually Bea's plants had taken over the whole backyard!

A loud creak and bang made me spin around. I got the feeling we were being watched. In the corner of my eye I thought I saw a white blur in the downstairs window. I couldn't exactly register what the blur looked like, but it made my heart thump. "Did you see that?" I asked Sookie.

Sookie had been bending over examining the petals of a strange purple plant when she slowly turned and said, "See what?"

I forced myself to check again. Nothing was there – except a desperate nagging inside me to get away.

Maybe I was overly paranoid, but this place was totally freaky. I dragged Sookie away and we headed home. That evening when Lea didn't show, I couldn't bring myself to go back to her place on my own and in the dark. I'd wait until school to talk to her.

***

Wednesday morning at breakfast Sookie seemed so hyper she was bouncing in her chair. She could barely eat her frosty oats and she quickly slurped back her orange juice. "Cat, can you take me to school this morning?"

This wasn't like my sister – she was not a morning person. "But I have to leave now to be at Mr. Keating's by 7:45. Wouldn't you rather wait and go with Mom later?"

A mysterious look shadowed Sookie's face, and she said, as if she was in a terrible hurry, "Mom's not ready and I have important errands."

What important errands could a nine-year-old have? But I just nodded. When I grabbed our backpacks off the hooks by the kitchen door, I noticed Sookie's backpack had an odd bulge, and for a moment, the shape reminded me of the creepy purple turban she used to wear. I'd thought for sure she'd left that at the Greystones'. "Hey, what's in here?"

Sookie reached into her bag and pulled out a blue wool hat that matched her coat. She had to have a hat for almost every occasion. At least this hat wasn't magical.

"There's nothing else inside but schoolwork," Sookie said as she cast a sly smile. "Your backpack doesn't bulge at all – shouldn't *it* be full of homework?"

Why did that set off a quiet alarm bell in my brain?

Mom came downstairs in a rush, tucking a white blouse into her plain wool skirt. Mom never wore cool bohemian clothes or fancy dresses like Lea's aunt. Then a guilty thought pinched me. She didn't have my option of getting a part-time job for a fancy outfit. All her money went to bills.

"Ooh, I'm running behind. Have either of you seen my maroon blouse? I couldn't find it anywhere this morning."

I shook my head. "Sorry ..."

"Hurry, Cat," Sookie said as she flew out the door.

After dropping Sookie off, I had to rush through work so I could still arrive early for school. I stood beside the drab grey lockers waiting for the other kids to shuffle in. Mr. Morrows and Ms. Dreeble had organized an early dance lesson because they had a staff meeting after school. This suited the girls as we'd planned to slip the boys the love charms while we danced.

If only I had a love charm to slip around Zach's neck.

This Valentine's dance wasn't turning out at all as I'd planned. I suddenly wondered how Lucinda's dance turned out all those years ago – if she managed to go to the dance with the popular boy, Roger. Still, I almost had my dress and now I hung out with lots of kids. I figured all I had to do was dodge Clive – who maybe was asking me out – and I'd probably end up having a good time at the dance with or without Zach. That is, as long as I sat out the ballroom dancing.

I'd put a lot of work into keeping everyone happy for the dance – so much so that …

Yikes – my science report. I hadn't even started it! I ran down the hall, then up the stairs. Maybe I could beg Ms. Dreeble for a little more time on my report. But when I reached the science room I hesitated by the open door. Sharp voices rose behind it.

"You said you'd meet me for dinner last night," I heard Mr. Morrows say. "You didn't answer your phone all day."

"I have a paper that's going to be published in *Scientific World*," said Ms. Dreeble. "I'm really sorry – I got so caught up in research and the deadline that I kept my phone off the hook and – "

"Forgot about me."

I stared at the yellowing linoleum as Mr. Morrows stormed out of the classroom past me.

Weird – I never exactly pictured my teachers having a life outside school. And I didn't know that Ms. Dreeble conducted real scientific research – that was cool. I tiptoed past the open door, but I couldn't resist peeking inside. Ms. Dreeble had put her head down on the desk.

"But I can't neglect my work ..." she said miserably.

I went by the office and said hi to Mom. She sat at her desk and I heard her muttering, "I checked my closet, every single drawer, *and* the laundry. How can a blouse just disappear?" When she finally noticed me, she waved in a distracted way.

By the time I got back down to the gym, the first thing that hit me was an overpowering smell of lavender and that darker odor. If there was a perfume called creepiness, it would smell like that. Right – all the girls would have their love charms ready to slip over the boys' heads. Yuck. The concoctions all smelled potent. Actually, they stank.

Mr. Morrows stood alone at the front of the gym looking like he'd much rather be coaching soccer as he began the music. It was weird thinking about him and Ms. Dreeble arguing.

"You never seem to focus on what you're doing," said Clive as he grabbed my hand. "Your head's always somewhere else."

I was about to come up with a smart reply such as, "Only when I'm stuck with you," but the smell in the gym got so pungent I began gagging.

"What's that stink," Clive complained.

However, most of the people in our class didn't seem to notice. Instead, they were dancing away as if nothing was peculiar. Well, not too peculiar. By the end of the dance the boys seemed to be just shuffling around. And when the bell finally rang, the boys only stopped dancing when the girls did. Then as the girls left the gym for their classes, the boys followed behind them almost like their shadows. I went up to science class.

"Cat," Ms. Dreeble said. "How is your report going? Don't forget it is due Monday, or you lose the bonus marks *and* I'll deduct work-habit marks," she said wearily. "You have a talent in science, Cat, and I expect you to do better."

That wasn't so bad …

"I'm thinking that report should include a bibliography," said Ms. Dreeble. "That shouldn't be too tough with all your extra time, should it?"

I nodded my head as my heart sank. Just what I needed, more work. I spent the lunch hour alone hauling out the rest of the Valentine's decorations and carrying them to the gym. All my friends, including Mia and Amarjeet, had forgotten about me as they hung around all the other girls at their lockers, giggling and talking. Oh, and they were surrounded by the boys!

"The love charms are awesome," whispered Amarjeet as Rabinder lingered by her with a lovesick smile.

"This was the best idea ever," Mia nodded in delight as Mitch grabbed her books to carry them home.

But the love charms shouldn't be working like this at all.

What was going on?

CHAPTER 15

A Grim Parade

AT LEAST LEA agreed to stay with me after school to hang all the Japanese lanterns and paper streamers for the dance. All the other girls had gone off with the boys and had deserted us. Lea didn't mention the night before, so when the moment seemed right, I asked, "What did you mean the other night? You seemed sort of ... upset," I finished awkwardly

But Lea only mumbled, "Well, I was worried about you getting in trouble." Which I had managed to do – well, almost. Then I grew quiet as I kept wondering how those silly love charms I'd made ended up having such a potent effect.

I reached into one of the boxes and pulled out that newspaper article again with the puzzling headline. *"Boy found ... still missing ..."* How can someone be lost and found at the same time? That's what I'd wanted to remember when Lucinda was telling us about her dance. If I'd described the photograph to her, maybe she'd have figured out what the headline was about. It had to be a well-known incident if it was on the front page of a newspaper. Or did it? I'd read papers before from back then, and it could have been that the kid lost his dog or something. Still, I was a bit curious. Folding the paper, I stuffed it in my jacket pocket.

It was getting late when I headed home, and I still had to stop to collect the last of my pay from Mr. Keating. By the time I stood in front of Esmeralda's shop window and stared again at my dream dress, some of my excitement had evaporated. Friday's dance was supposed to be an awesome event with me wearing the coolest dress.

I was beginning to realize it wasn't going to play out that way – mostly due to the fact that my friends all went home with the boys of their dreams trailing after them. It wasn't bugging me that I'd be the only girl without a partner. As much as I wanted to believe everything was normal in this town, boys didn't really fall under a love charm of crushed lavender and catnip, even if girls wished for that to happen under a storm moon.

Are there ever any happy endings?

Just then, Esmeralda spotted me and came outside as the bell above her door clanged. "So are you here to pick up the dress?"

"I guess."

"I expect more enthusiasm than that," said Esmeralda as she stared at my navy velour track suit that sort of rode up my waist. She had my dress neatly packed between tissue paper and had enclosed it in a cardboard box. "This dress will be the most exquisite one at the Valentine's dance. I love Valentine's day, it's so romantic."

"Um, yeah." I noticed the way Esmeralda kept looking out the window. She was staring at Mr. Keating again, who stood in front of his apple barrel holding a Valentine card. He was gazing off into nowhere with an eerie, vacant stare. I noticed a flash of red under his apron, and a balloon of worry began inflating in my stomach.

I thanked Esmeralda and slipped my boxed dress under my arm. I bumped into a few grown-ups as they shuffled down the street – usually I was the one caught up in daydreams and distractions. They had the same weird stare as Mr. Keating. What was up with everyone? I headed home thinking whatever weirdness was going on, it had better not wreck the dance. When I turned down the last street, I spotted Lea hanging over her fence talking to Jasper. She waved for me to come over and join them; she'd been so quiet when we were decorating the gym, and she wasn't exactly smiling now.

"You must really like the scarf I gave you because that's, like, the third time I've seen you wear it," Lea said as she managed a half-smile.

That was a bit embarrassing, but it was true. I loved my – um, her – pink scarf. I'd wear it every day if I could, but I was trying to keep it nice for the dance.

"Hey, I'm coming over to your place later," she brightened. "Your mom and my aunt are having coffee. Uh, maybe you shouldn't wear the scarf then. It's just that … my aunt might not approve of me lending it to you."

"Don't worry." I understood because Mom never liked me borrowing anything, as it just wouldn't do to accidentally lose it or damage it. "But I'm wearing it to the dance on Friday if it's okay."

"Totally," Lea said.

"The dance," Jasper said in a disgusted way. "What a stupid idea the whole thing is."

Wow, it wasn't like my friend to be so negative. And yet, I was starting to feel ... "What's wrong?" I asked him softly.

Lea piped up, "Jasper had worked on some amazing poems for a Valentine to a girl, and she didn't even open it. She just went on and on about going to the dance with some other boy."

That would be Mia, I thought.

Lea looked sympathetically at Jasper. "I'd have gone with you in a second," she said.

Jasper looked happier. Too bad Lea wasn't allowed to go. I shrugged and said, "Yeah, the whole dance thing is getting ..." my voice trailed off. I spotted a peculiar sight that made me do a triple-take.

Most of our soccer team was walking down my street – first the girls and then the boys, who were trailing behind them. And they were heading to my house!

"I should check out what's going on," I said as I broke out in a run, pointing to the straggling parade of kids.

Jasper hesitated. "Are you coming?" he asked Lea.

"Can't," she said. "I'm waiting for my aunt." She checked nervously over her shoulder at her house that sat in the yard like a lurking beast. I pulled Lea's scarf tighter around me and started running again. Jasper and I raced back to my place.

When we approached my house, a bunch of kids were standing on our sidewalk, and some of them had lined up on the steps. Our front door was open and Sookie stood on the porch. Jasper and I pushed our way through the crowd until we joined Sookie. Buddy was perched on her shoulder, twitching his little nose as he checked out the crowd.

"Will you get Rabinder to go home?" Amarjeet said in an exasperated voice. "He won't talk and he won't listen. All he does is follow me everywhere, and my mom is getting angry."

Rabinder stood beside Amarjeet wearing a vacant grin on his face. Every time Amarjeet climbed a step toward us, he climbed one. If she stepped back, he stepped back. "It has to be the love charm," she said shaking her head.

"Maybe there *can* be too much of a good thing," Mia said giving Mitch a gentle shove and turning him to face in the opposite direction. He'd been leaning over her from behind, and a thin line of drool had dripped from his mouth and onto her shoulder. He wore the same vacant stare.

"This is definitely not cool," complained Emily. She turned in disgust to watch Zach flit from Amanda to Ashley to Jennifer like a confused moth banging up against a light bulb.

As I lay my dress box down on the porch, Sookie's eyes grew wider and wider. "Cat," she said. "I think we have a problem."

Every single boy who wore a love charm was following a girl around in big shuffling steps and acting as is if there wasn't a single thought in his head other than to be her shadow. Horrified, I stared at the guys' identical stupid grins, as the only thing their eyes tracked was the girl right in front of them. Except for Zach who wore five love charms. As a result, he kept shuffling aimlessly from girl to girl.

"What have you done?" cried Jasper.

"Nothing," I squeaked. "I created love charms, but only with lavender and catnip and ordinary herbs. It was all supposed to be fun."

"But Cat," Sookie began.

"Take them off," I said quickly. "Take off their love charms."

"Won't they get ... mad at us," Mia said as she frowned.

"You should have thought about that earlier," Jasper said in a harsh tone.

"I already tried that," complained Amarjeet. "The charm won't come off."

Emily went over and tugged at the red sachet that hung around Zach's neck. "Nope," she said. "It won't budge." Then she yanked even harder until poor Zach was making a sort of choking sound.

"Easy," cried Amanda as she pulled Emily back.

"This can't be happening." I was totally confused.

"Cat," Sookie began again.

"What?" I snapped impatiently. My kid sister dragged me into our hallway and whispered, "When you weren't looking I sort of added extra ingredients to your love charms."

"What kind of ingredients?" The worry balloon kept inflating, making my stomach even tighter.

"The mullein stuff and Spanish moss, and um, licorice root," Sookie said as she grew paler and paler. "I didn't think it would make the charms this strong."

"Why?" I gasped. "Sookie, why would you use

magic when I specifically told you not to?"

Sookie started snuffling. "'Cause your stuff wouldn't work. I tried to tell you that."

"But I didn't want it to work – not magically," I whispered frantically.

"A little help here," Amarjeet called through the door.

Sookie hung her head. "Cat, your friends would have been mad. You wanted them to like you. I was just trying to help. And Aunt Bea told me those ingredients would make the charms more potent."

I glared at her as my skin crawled with goose bumps. Did Bea have something to do with this catastrophe? I should have believed my first instincts when she and Sookie had gone off to admire her stupid plants. But there was no time to think about that at the moment.

"First, she's not your aunt. Second, in case you haven't noticed, my friends are pretty mad."

"Well, this is a real predicament," was all Sookie said as she went into the living room and tucked Buddy inside his hamster ball.

Yeah, no kidding. I went back onto the porch wondering what to do next. For a few moments the only sound was the spinning of Buddy's ball as it clattered across the floor.

"If we can't take the charms off," I said suddenly, "we could cut the conjure bags and let the herbs *fall* out." I ran into the kitchen to grab scissors. When I got back onto the porch, the girls had lined the boys up in a row waiting for me. Taking Rabinder's red silk conjure bag into my hand, I carefully began to slice it open. But the bag quickly slid from my fingers and I almost cut myself.

I dropped the scissors.

It was as if whatever was inside those crimson bags was alive.

CHAPTER 16

A Terrible Twist

"AMARJEET," I GULPED nervously. "Hold the bag for me."

Amarjeet grimaced, but she reached for the bag and grasped it. "Don't stab my fingers."

Again, even more carefully this time, I opened the scissors to begin snipping. The bag squirmed; Amarjeet shrieked and drew back her hand.

"What's going on down there," Mom called from her bedroom. "I'm trying to take a nap before dinner."

Please don't come down, please don't come down, I pleaded in my mind. "Nothing," I called back. Then as calmly as I could, I suggested, "Mom, why don't you rest a few more minutes, and I'll turn on the oven to get things started." Taking my cue, Sookie took off to do just that.

She came back in a snap and shouted, "Done," before she caught her breath.

"Thanks," Mom said. "I'll be down in about fifteen minutes."

I leaned closer to Rabinder. "Can you hear me at all?"

"Ugh," he replied.

"Zach," I said. He stopped and hovered for a second when I called his name. "Do you know where you are?"

"Ugh."

"So they seem to be following basic questions," I

122

said hopefully.

"Will you boys go home ... please," Amarjeet said in desperation.

"Ugh," Rabinder grunted, and he started to leave, but he hesitated, looking confused about which direction to go.

Oh crap. Now what?

"Take them home," said Jasper to the girls. "Set them up in front of a computer game or the television. That shouldn't be too challenging for them. And as long as they do as they're told, maybe their parents won't notice anything until Cat can figure out how to get rid of the charm."

Unless they're asked to do something complicated like setting the table, I thought. It wasn't a great plan, but at least it was a plan.

Each girl took a boy's hand and set off to deliver him home. A long straggling zombie parade marched out of our yard and down the street.

"You'd better pick them up tomorrow morning and take them to school," I warned the girls.

Jasper and I sat down on the porch steps, and I placed my head in my hands.

I told Jasper about Sookie sneaking extra ingredients into my love charms. My sister found this a convenient time to put Buddy back in his hamster cage up in her room. She said she didn't want him to catch a cold.

"How did Sookie learn so much about magical plants and potions?" Jasper asked.

"From Lea's aunt," I said. "Bea seems so kind, but I'm starting to think that there's a reason I get a creepy feeling whenever I'm at Lea's house, or when I'm around her aunt."

"What do you mean?" asked Jasper in a way that made me wonder if he sensed something wasn't quite right about them as well.

"The house is ugly on the outside, but nice and exotic on the inside," I mused. "Lea's aunt always seems so nice, and she looks so attractive on the outside … but …" I didn't want to say she seemed ugly on the inside, so I just said, "There's darkness there."

"What about Lea?" Jasper said softly.

"I'm worried about her," I confessed. "I think she's afraid of her aunt."

"She did seem quiet earlier." Concern crept into Jasper's voice. "But why would Lea's aunt trick Sookie into turning those boys into zombies," Jasper pondered with disgust.

"I keep thinking it's got something to do with our Valentine's dance." My mind began racing. "And the dance Lucinda attended seventy years ago," I said, pulling the crumpled newspaper out of my pocket. My eyes ran across those headlines again about a boy missing and found. That didn't make sense, but alarm bells clanged in my head. It doesn't add up – Lucinda doesn't remember much, so how can she be sure her dance had really turned out okay …"

"Maybe you're looking at this the wrong way," said Jasper as if deep in thought.

"What do you mean?" I asked.

"What if the dance was just an event and what mattered was the time of year on the – "

"Celtic calendar," I gasped. Of course! During certain times of the year life got more dangerous on Grim Hill. Humans are more vulnerable against fairies when the veil that separates our world and theirs becomes thinner – that's when fairy magic can slip into our lives and cause trouble. The Celts, who lived in Europe a couple thousand years ago, didn't have much science or technology. But what they understood perfectly were fairies – and how you had to watch out for them.

I ran upstairs and came down with a stack of books given to me by Forenza, the niece of Alice and Lucinda. I wasn't able to return them to her as she'd fled our town after the last close encounter with fairies.

If only I could do the same right now.

Jasper and I began flipping through pages. "Look," Jasper said pointing to a page. "February is the time of year the Celts held their festival of Imbolic."

"We had fairy trouble during Samhain and a close call during the winter solstice," I said worriedly, "but Lucinda said Grim Hill is locked tight now. I think she'd know." After spending seventy years inside a Fairy hill, Lucinda was very sensitive to Grim magic.

"Imbolic doesn't sound too dangerous." Jasper scanned the pages as I stood over his shoulder trying to keep up. "It seems the Celts wanted to prepare for spring crops, so they built bonfires and passed through them hoping to leave ill fortune behind and bring in good luck. Then they used the ashes to sprinkle and purify the ground." Jasper rubbed his head, which was always a sign he was deep in thought.

"The Celts were smart," he said after a moment.

"Ashes also make good fertilizer for the soil. It would help their crops grow."

Growing plants – nothing was growing as fast as Sookie's stupid plants, and that's what got us into this mess. Still, I couldn't connect all the dots. "Does it mention fairy trouble anywhere?"

"No, not during Imbolic," said Jasper. "Not like when there was the Celtic festival of Samhain or the winter solstice."

There had to be a link to what was happening now and this Celtic festival, but what was it? "Sookie's been very particular about the moon – whether it's a storm moon or a gibbous moon," I added. "Is there anything in these books about storm moons and Imbolic?"

Jasper flipped more pages. "Oh."

That didn't sound good. As I scanned, I read that the Celtic calendar was based on the moon phases. Then, a passage at the bottom of the page sent chills along my neck and back as if I was rubbing up against an iceberg.

"The storm moon is also known as the hunger moon during Imbolic," I finally said. "Creatures who have been hibernating awaken and creep out of their lairs looking to feed."

"You mean like bears?" Sookie had finally returned.

Jasper and I nodded, but both of us knew I didn't mean bears. Fairies drained humans of their life force – that was like feeding ...

"Sookie, do you know how to undo the charm?" I tried sounding calm. "Can you turn everyone back to normal?" Maybe we could fix this.

"Not exactly," said Sookie. Then she brightened. "I

could ask Aunt Bea."

"No," Jasper and I said at once.

"There's something else I should tell you, Cat." Sookie looked guilty. That balloon kept inflating making my stomach ache big-time.

"I sort of made new conjure bags from Mom's blouse." Sookie gave a little sniff. "That's why I needed to get to school early. I ... I ...set up a chair and table in the schoolyard and sold my valentine charms."

"What?" My head began to spin. "Why?"

Sookie's eyes glistened as she looked at me. "Kind of like last summer, Cat, when you helped me set up a lemonade stand. Only this time, lots of people wanted to buy the charms." She sniffed again. "I was selling them because I wanted a part-time job like you."

"Lots of people? Don't you mean kids?" I asked, but my heart pounded. I remembered the flash of red I'd seen beneath Mr. Keating's apron, and I recalled the other adults who had been shuffling down the street.

Sookie shook her head. "Most of my friends didn't want to buy a valentine charm," she said with a scowl. "They don't like romance either. But parents bought charms on their way to work, and so did a few teachers and passersby."

Jasper turned pale. I gulped. "How many did you sell?" I asked.

"Fifteen dollars worth," said Sookie. "At fifty cents each, that's, um ..." Even though my sister was a master magician and had a way with words, she still only knew grade three arithmetic.

"Thirty bags," I said miserably.

"Oh, hello, Jasper," said Mom. "So what have you three been up to?"

"Nothing," we all said at once.

"What's this?" Mom picked up the box I'd dumped on the porch and opened it. "Oh," her voice sounded flat. "So that's why you wanted a part-time job," Mom said in a quiet way that managed to make my stomach twist even more.

"I like the outfit you're making me," I said quickly, "but ..." There were too many things going on at the moment, and I couldn't think of the right way to tell her about the dress. I'd blown it by not asking her about it earlier, but she didn't lecture me. She just kept holding the box and looking at me. Somehow, that was worse.

"Mom, could we talk about this later?" I glanced at Jasper.

Mom, thinking I didn't want to argue in front of my friend, simply said, "I guess so, Cat," as if she didn't care that much. Instead of being relieved, a lump formed in my chest, but I had to go.

Promising to talk to her about the dress later, I made an abrupt exit and hurried with Jasper to the Greystones. Lucinda just had to remember more about her Valentine's dance ... we had to gather all the pieces of this puzzle and put them together fast. We pounded on the doorknocker, and for the first time when Alice opened the door, she didn't greet us with her warm smile. In fact, she looked terrible.

"Oh, my dears," Alice said as she wrung her hands. "I'm just on my way to the hospital. Lucinda has taken ill and she collapsed. I'm so sorry, but I have to rush away.

My poor sister." Alice sounded miserable.

I thought about how frail Lucinda seemed the last time I saw her, and dread seeped inside me just when I thought I couldn't feel worse. All we could do was bring Lucinda's suitcase to the car, and stand helplessly on the curb and wave goodbye.

"Lucinda will get better," I said in a cheery tone that I knew Jasper didn't believe. I wasn't sure I was even convincing myself. "In the meantime I'll just have to get Lea alone tonight and ask her more about her aunt," I said, although my heart filled with alarm. "And I'll keep a very close eye on Bea."

"I'll hit the books and the internet," said Jasper who'd thrown most of my books in his bag back at my house. "Be careful, Cat."

And as if to drive that home, a blood curdling wail unfurled in the night.

CHAPTER 17

The Mask Slips

THE KITCHEN CLOCK ticked second by second, minute by slow, agonizing minute. Nine girls on our soccer team had turned the boys into zombies thanks to my brilliant idea. And Sookie had sold thirty more love charms. We were in deep.

"You don't seem particularly hungry," Mom said as she glanced at my dinner; I'd barely touched my food. "I thought you liked turkey burgers."

"About the dress ..." I began, but Mom cut me off.

"Cat, it's your money, you earned it. I just hope you get enough satisfaction from it. After all, that money could have gone a long way." Then Mom smiled more kindly and said, "Eat your dinner, honey."

Staring at the burger reminded me of the boys and how they now had the brain of a turkey. I tried taking a bite, but it tasted like sawdust. Sookie, on the other hand, happily chomped away.

"You better take *your* money and buy Mom a new blouse," I whispered harshly. That was all I could think to say because none of this was exactly Sookie's fault. She'd meant well, but she had to learn that her powers had consequences.

Sookie nodded weakly and put her burger down. I took another small bite and chewed as the seconds dragged out even longer. What if Lea wouldn't tell me anything about her aunt, or what if all the boys stayed zombies forever and … and … *Stop*, I told myself. *One step at a time.*

If only each step didn't seem to last forever.

After I dried the last plate and placed it in the cupboard, the doorbell rang. I dropped the tea towel on the floor and raced for the door. Of course, Sookie beat me to it and was already inviting Lea and her aunt inside.

Bea was wearing a stunning silk dress in the palest grey, and her long blond hair flowed over her shoulders in gleaming waves. She appeared so different from Mom who was in her faded jeans and had her hair pinned back in a tidy bun "I'll put coffee on," Mom said.

"For us too?" asked Lea.

"Certainly not," Mom laughed. "But I'll tell you what, I'll throw a few marshmallows into your hot chocolate."

My cheeks should have burned with embarrassment because Mom wasn't hip and she treated us like little kids, but instead it created warmth inside me and a longing to be a little kid again. I followed her into the kitchen and blurted out, "Mom, could we move from this stupid town? Could we *please* go back to the city?"

"What? Don't be silly, Cat. You know better. The rent is much cheaper here, and besides, things are going well with my night classes, and look at all your friends. Even Sookie seems to be thriving."

Blood drained from my face. She had that right.

"Is something wrong?" Mom put her hands on my shoulders and looked at me in alarm. "You know you can tell me anything, sweetie."

Tell my mom that an evil zombie enchantment lurked right under her nose? Tell her that her youngest child was a powerful magician that wreaked havoc by accident? That maybe the kind lady she'd invited for coffee was someone wicked? Yeah. "Nothing's wrong," I said. "I just miss our old life."

Mom's smile tightened as if it was pasted on her face, and I suspected she missed that life as well.

"But you're right," I said and hoped I sounded cheerier. "Things are going well." I grabbed the milk and sugar tray and hurried to the coffee table so she wouldn't see that my cheeks were burning now.

Before I could get Lea alone to ask about her aunt, Sookie asked, "Would everyone like to see my garden?"

"Definitely," said Bea.

Wary of Bea's dark influence on my sister, I followed them outside.

Sookie's plants now looked like plant-people with their bobbing flower heads stretching their leafy arms up to the moonlight. I shuddered and looked away.

"How odd," Mom said in an almost dreamy voice.

"This is an *astonishing* garden," Bea said slowly with a smile that I could now see had a cruel hook. "You are very ... talented."

Sookie beamed, but Lea, who'd been extremely quiet since she'd arrived, gulped. Her eyes darted constantly toward her aunt.

"Why don't you take Lea to meet Buddy," I said to Sookie.

Sookie had already grabbed Lea's hand and was half dragging her upstairs, so I had to rush after them –

anxious to talk once we were out of Bea and Mom's hearing range. After we stepped through the piles of clothes, shoes, and toys that cluttered Sookie's floor, Lea fiddled with Buddy's equally messy hamster cage.

"Lea," I began, "remember how you told me about lavender and yarrow being good for romance? Do you know how to, well, undo love charms?"

"Why don't you let me ask Aunt ..." Sookie started to say, but I glared at her and whispered for her to hush.

Lea shot me a frightened look, but I wasn't sure if it was because she knew we were in trouble, or if she was afraid to help us. She picked up one of Sookie's stuffed dolls and hugged it to her chest and said, "Say a love charm was set by a storm moon, it might dissolve after the dark moon rises. Except ..."

"Except what?" I didn't like how Lea's face twisted with dread.

Lea's face twisted some more, and I suddenly realized it was because she was trying to tell me something, but her lips were frozen and her mouth had been locked up. As if someone had hit me in the stomach, it was all I could do not to double over. I'd seen something like that before at Halloween when Lucinda had tried to reveal how to break the link to Fairy, but fairy magic had locked her mouth tight.

"What's wrong with Lea?" Sookie whispered urgently in my ear. She then said, "Lea, say something."

As Lea struggled to talk, a quiet terror made me dizzy. If my hair wasn't already streaked with green, it would be streaking grey from worry, just like Mom said was happening to her hair – but unlike Mom, I wasn't joking.

"Cat?" Sookie said in a frightened voice.

Lea moaned in pain. Sookie cried out, "What's happening?"

"Some kind of fairy magic," I said to Lea and Sookie. "A magic that's freezing your mouth shut, right Lea?"

Of course Lea couldn't answer, but she nodded and her eyes didn't show surprise.

Sookie studied Lea and her little face dimpled with deep thought. "Give Lea one of *your* possessions, Cat."

"What do you mean?" I asked.

"Just try it, hurry."

I rushed into my room and grabbed a clean pair of socks Mom had bundled on my dresser. I ran back to Sookie's room, handing them to Lea. She clutched the socks in her hand.

"I ... I'm okay now. That was close. If my aunt found out I was trying to ..." Lea took a deep breath. "Be careful, Cat. Be really careful."

"Careful of what?" I asked as terror seeped into my blood.

Lea widened her eyes as her mouth opened and closed, but words didn't come out until she shook her head, warning me not to ask questions. "Just keep your guard up – watch out for your friends. I ... better go. Um, can I keep your socks? One of your possessions might help me sometime."

Keep my socks? I'd grabbed the first thing I saw, but Lea had been generous with me ... and I got the feeling I should pay back in kind. What did I have that was as special as the scarf she'd given me? Lea always wore green. Ah, I knew what I had to give to my friend.

I went and rifled through my closet and brought out the soccer jersey I'd worn for the Grimoire Halloween match. I'd loved that jersey with the black and green stripes, but I didn't have much use for the shirt anymore. The match ended in disaster, and the school didn't even exist anymore. I raced back to Sookie's room.

"Would you like my soccer shirt instead?" I asked. "It's the perfect color for you. With my hair this way," I pointed to my streaks, "it seems a bit too green for me now."

Lea's eyes teared up and she put on my jersey. "No one has ever given me anything before," her words burst out at last. "Oh, Cat. Please promise me no matter what, *you'll wear my scarf to the dance*. Promise?"

"Sure, the scarf goes perfectly with my new dress." What was Lea trying to tell me? She knew I wanted to wear the scarf with my dress anyway.

"No matter what." Lea shook her head. "Don't forget."

"I promise," I said. Then she pulled her fancy cashmere sweater over the jersey and fled the room.

What just happened? I wandered down the stairs as Lea rushed out the door. Mom and Bea had finished their coffee and Bea said, "Well, I guess that's my signal to go home."

I stood with Sookie on the porch as Bea and Lea walked down our front path. When they crossed under a street light, the yellow fluorescent glare turned Bea's face first into a young girl's face that was strangely familiar, and then in a flash it morphed into a Halloween mask of scars and wrinkles. I gasped, but the image only lasted a second.

"Did you see that?" I asked my sister, half hoping she saw that her "auntie" was something evil, but half hoping she'd been spared the horrific sight.

Except Sookie nodded saying, "Bea is a wicked fairy."

I'd thought Bea had magical abilities like my sister, but I thought she was human, even when I suspected her magic had become dark. But if she was a fairy … My poor friend. My heart broke for Lea.

"Don't you know?" Sookie turned to me. "Lea's a fairy, too."

What?

But even as my head whirled, I understood one thing. When it came to fairy stuff, Sookie knew.

CHAPTER 18
A Dark Hunger Awakens ...

ALL THAT NIGHT I wondered if there were good fairies. None of them had been good so far ... except that one time when the Oak King had helped me as payment for a favor. Could Lea be good? I twisted in my blankets and kicked off my quilt. Could Lea be evil? I twisted the other way and tangled myself in my sheets. It didn't help that there was a constant eerie wailing outside my window and by morning, every hair stood on my head and goose bumps rippled all over my arms. Then I had to go to school, even though I now fully understood something terrible was going on.

I met up with Jasper and I told him the news about Lea and her aunt and how they were fairies.

"No, not Lea," Jasper sounded crushed. "Are you sure, Cat?"

"Sookie is sure." Both Jasper and I understood Sookie had an uncanny sense about fairy things. But was Lea evil? I didn't think so. I was sure Lea was trying to help me. Maybe some fairies weren't as wicked as the others. At least, that's what I tried to tell myself.

We split up once we reached school, and I agreed to keep an eye on the zombies and see if I could figure out how they'd all react to the dance tomorrow night. Jasper would skip the dance lessons after school and do more

Celtic research.

As I sat in science class, I watched with growing dread as Ms. Dreeble slumped at her desk and kept opening and closing her yellow binder. She'd stare at us, begin her lecture, "Today class ... we're going to ..." then she'd sit back down and flip through her book. But instead of reading anything, she'd stare off into the distance.

We all sat uncomfortably in our seats wondering what to do next. Then I spotted something on Ms. Dreeble's desk that made me gasp.

"What?" Mia said suspiciously.

"Oh, nothing ... I just um ... dropped my pen." I bent over as if I was looking for it.

Even when the noise level began to rise, Ms. Dreeble didn't care that we were all chatting with each other. That is, Amanda and Mia were complaining to each other and ignoring me. So were a bunch of the other girls. Mitch and Rabinder sat in their seats staring straight ahead. I wished Mitch would stop drooling – not that Ms. Dreeble noticed.

When the bell rang, I lingered behind until the rest of the kids left. Then I casually sauntered up to Ms. Dreeble's desk. "My essay is going great," I told her – though that was only an excuse to get closer to her, I hadn't touched my assignment yet.

"Um ... hmm ... ah ..." Ms. Dreeble kept flipping through her book.

I left but I'd seen enough. A paper valentine decorated in liberal swipes of red sparkle-pen – specially designed by Sookie – sat on my teacher's desk. Inside the card was signed by Mr. Morrows and a tell-tale fragment of red thread was still taped onto the card. Ms. Dreeble had taken her Valentine's charm and put it in a pocket or something. She too had been turned into a zombie.

During our dance lessons that day, Ms. Dreeble stood in front of the gym opening and shutting her mouth, blinking her eyes, and just staring straight ahead. When Mr. Morrows announced they'd give a demonstration of how to do a waltz turn, she only shuffled around.

I was staring at them so hard I fumbled the next dance step.

"Wow," said Clive. He ran his fingers through his black curly hair. "Even with you missing that step, we're still the best dancers in the whole class today."

No kidding, I thought. Every girl had anticipated the dance so much, and now they all had mindless zombies for partners. Not to mention they had to deliver the boys to school, to each class, and back home again. The girls would be exhausted by tomorrow night. Some Valentine's dance this was going to be for them. I winced as Mia sent a scathing glare my way. They all blamed me.

"Glad I have your undivided attention," Clive said sarcastically.

"Sorry, what's that again?" The lesson was passing in slow agony.

"I said," Clive almost shouted as if I was dumb instead of uninterested, "too bad there isn't a prize for the best ballroom dancers – we'd win."

"You're not even dancing tomorrow night," I reminded him. "Your band is playing."

"And won't that be a waste of my talent," he said in disgust as he watched everyone stumble and collide with each other. "About the dance, I've been meaning to ask if after the dance, we could, I mean … you'd be my …"

Before Clive could ask me something I suspected I didn't want to hear, I broke away saying I had to meet up with Jasper. Clive looked disappointed, but I fumed. Trust Clive not to even notice his friends were zombies. He was so full of himself.

Jasper wasn't at his locker so I had to search the school until I found him in the library. He'd been pouring through Forenza's Celtic mythology book.

He looked up at me and said, "How are the …"

"Zombies?" I whispered. "Pretty much the same, but Lea had said the charm could maybe be dissolved under a dark moon. But I'm not sure what she meant. Did you find out anything?"

I didn't like the look on Jasper's face.

"I cross-referenced the Celtic festival, Imbolic, and fairies, Cat, but I could only come up with one connection."

"What's that?" I asked almost afraid to hear the answer. As if a cloud blocked the window, the room grew darker. And Darkmont's library, with its dingy venetian blinds and grey-lined walls containing tattered books, seemed dark enough.

Jasper opened his book to a page illustrated with a blond Celtic queen. "Candlemas and St. Brigit's Day are other names for the February festival of Imbolic."

Candlemas. I leaned closer. I had learned – the hard way – that the Celts typically used fire or light to battle fairy enchantments. "Did you find a way to undo the Valentine's charms?"

"No," Jasper shook his head.

That simple word made me brace myself. "What did you find?"

"The Celtic goddess, Brigit, is called a fairy in some legends. She reigns during Imbolic and she can appear young or very old."

"Like Lea's aunt," I said, thinking of the ancient hag I'd seen under the streetlight. Come to think of it, that was the frightful vision I'd seen in the window of Lea's house during the storm. Probably Skeeter had seen it too the way he went on about seeing a witch there.

"But Lea's aunt is a fairy not a Celtic goddess," I said trying to see the connection.

Jasper squirmed uncomfortably in his chair. "Some of these myths say Brigit was the first banshee. That's where everything matches up – fairies, Valentine's, and storm moons."

Banshee. Thoughts spun around in my head. What did I know about banshees? They were scary – why? Something about sounding like a banshee – right – wailing and screeching ... because ... because ... "Isn't a banshee," I began slowly, "a creature who wails and screams when someone is about to die?" I swallowed, but it was more like a gulp.

Then we both grew silent as a harsh wailing screeched like a siren in the distance. The same screeching that had been going on night after night.

"Cat," Jasper said suddenly. "Do you think someone is going to die?"

A cold chill settled over me as I shook my head. "Does that book tell us anything else about banshees?"

"Some myths state the banshee can be a supernatural creature that feeds on the souls of young men to keep herself young forever," Jasper said sounding puzzled.

"Under February's storm moon a dark hunger looks to feed," I said as the puzzle pieces began snapping together. I didn't like the picture. "Fine, my new best friend might be related to a banshee, except I don't see how it's Lea's fault, whether she is a fairy or not." I leaned over to read the page Jasper was holding, but he slammed the book shut.

"The rest only mentions how banshees often wear grey," said Jasper. "Bea always wears grey, right?"

I nodded in agreement. "I sensed danger way back, you know. Even their house didn't add up, the way it appeared decrepit on the outside but fantastical on the inside – with rich tapestries and silk banners and exotic carpets and glowing lamps." I struggled trying to figure out Lea's place. "Like the inside of a fortuneteller's tent at a carnival, cool and exciting but ..."

"But what?" asked Jasper.

"Whenever I was there, I couldn't wait to leave. The house gave me the creeps. As if it was haunted."

Jasper shook his head. "Part decrepit and eerie and part beautiful – that sounds a lot like a magical place, don't you think?"

Like Fairy.

We sat in silence for a minute, both of us thinking how we'd missed the obvious. *Get a grip*, I told myself as my brain shouted, *Why didn't you see that?*

"Cat," said Jasper. "I'm not sure, but I think there might be one more connection. There's a bit in one book about a 'sweetheart fairy,' a type of banshee that lures young men to their doom. And 'sweetheart' sounds like it could be about Valentines, right? And the Irish name for banshee sounds a bit like Bea's name.

"I'm not exactly following you." It was as if my brain didn't want to make any more dreadful connections.

"What is Bea's last name?" prompted Jasper in an odd whisper.

I thought back to the first day Lea came to class and Ms. Dreeble asked her to spell her name. "Shea," I said, narrowing my eyes. "Bea ... Shea ... yeah, so?"

"Celtic for banshee is Bea-Ann-Shea," Jasper concluded.

Ann – wasn't that the name of the girl at Lucinda's dance seventy years ago? The blond-haired girl who went off with Gordie? I thought about the face I'd seen under my street lamp as Bea had changed from girl to woman to hag. I felt inside my jacket pocket and pulled out the old newspaper clipping of the curly haired boy and blond girl. Could there be an even bigger link to our Valentine's dance than Jasper realized?

Blood thundered in my ears as I stared at the picture. "No way."

CHAPTER 19

A Dark Visit

JUMPING UP FROM the table, I began to pace. "I *have* to talk to Lucinda. She said there was no connection between her dance and ours, but something's clouding her memory – something she's *forgotten*, and we need to know."

I tried to make it sound as if my heart wasn't pounding so hard that blood buzzed in my ears.

Jasper didn't disagree with me about questioning Lucinda, but he didn't say it was a good idea either. As a matter of fact, Jasper was strangely quiet. I couldn't blame him – Lucinda wasn't well. But we had to figure out what the banshee was after and how that was tied to the dance tomorrow night.

This time we didn't pound on the Greystones' door-knocker. We tapped it gently. It took awhile, but Alice finally opened.

"Shh," she said, but she smiled. "My sister's back from the hospital, but she's resting upstairs. The doctor says her heart is weak."

"I need to ask Lucinda a question," I said. "It might upset her."

"Oh Cat, that would be too dangerous right now," said Alice.

"We think a banshee has come to our town,"

Jasper said.

"And the same banshee may have visited seventy years ago – when Lucinda had her Valentine's dance."

Alice Greystone didn't say "What nonsense," nor did she shoo us away. Instead she nodded slowly as worry blossomed on her face, and she ushered us in as we explained about Sookie crafting love charms that turned the boys into zombies – that she'd got the idea from Bea, and why we thought Bea might be a banshee. Neither Jasper nor I mentioned Lea. We knew none of this was her fault.

Although Alice looked worried and sad, she said, "Well, we can't very well stand back and let something terrible happen. Lucinda wouldn't want that."

We crept up the staircase with the mahogany banister, and when Alice tapped lightly on the bedroom door and opened it, I could smell camphor and cough syrup. Alice went in first while Jasper and I waited in the hall as I shifted my stocking feet on the braided rug.

"Cat, Jasper, please come in, " Alice called.

Lucinda lay in a dark four poster bed, her white lace coverlet and white nightgown providing a stark contrast against the black headboard. She sat propped up on several white satin pillows. It disturbed me to see her skin almost as pale as the bedsheet.

"I'm sorry, Cat," Lucinda said in a voice as fragile as tissue paper. "Alice told me why you are both here. I've tried and I've tried, but I cannot remember the night of my Valentine's dance."

"If you wouldn't mind, perhaps this would help." I handed the folded newspaper clipping to Lucinda.

Lucinda clutched the paper in her hand and as she smoothed it out and stared at the picture, she grew paler. Alice had been standing close by, and she quickly poured her sister a glass of water and fussed over her lace bedcover. Lucinda stared at the photograph and the jumbled headlines for a long time.

"It is guilt that made me forget," Lucinda said at last as she handed me back the newspaper. Her face grew tragic. "I remember what those headlines said. They're about a terrible secret that I've kept buried deep inside."

Alice reached over and held her sister's hand. "What is it?"

Then in that faraway voice Lucinda had used when she retold the night of the dance, she began:

"After I'd turned Gordie down so cruelly, he began following Ann everywhere. I thought they had become good friends. But Gordie didn't show up at the dance with Ann. He didn't show up at the dance with anyone. I went to the dance with Roger, and I remember how beautiful the gymnasium looked with the glowing red lanterns as we danced in the swirling crimson light. But halfway through the event we heard a terrible wail and then a scream. It cut through the music, and the fun everyone was having evaporated on the spot. A deep sadness hung over us all like a black veil."

A tear trailed down Lucinda's cheek. "After the dance poor Gordie's lifeless body was found near the school at the foot of Grim Hill. That's what the headline said: 'Young boy found dead, girl still missing.'"

My chest squeezed until it hurt. I almost fainted.

"What happened to Ann then?" Jasper said nervously from where he stood over in the corner of the room. I was pretty sure I knew, but I waited for Lucinda to speak again.

Lucinda closed her eyes. "I'm sure Ann was never seen again. But of course I would disappear from our town in a few short months. Do you recall seeing Ann again?" Lucinda asked Alice, but Alice shook her head.

"I never told anyone how I'd been cruel to Gordie and how he chose instead to be with Ann that night." Lucinda hung her head. "Now I fear I led him to his doom. That's why I couldn't ... didn't ... want to remember such a terrible secret."

"You couldn't have known what would happen to Gordie," comforted Alice.

"And you couldn't have known Ann was a banshee," I said, explaining the girl in the picture had the same face I'd seen on Bea when it melted and changed under the streetlight.

But Lucinda didn't want comfort. As if releasing her guilty secret eased her worried heart, her color deepened, and she said, "We cannot let what happened to Gordie happen to anyone else. Who might this banshee be after?" Lucinda paused as if she was trying to use just the right words. "Cat, is there someone you may have spurned?"

"Spurned?"

"A boy who you've rejected," said Lucinda as she winced with guilt. "A young man who is feeling alone in this world could be drawn to a banshee's lure."

My face got hot and I said, "Sort of ... maybe. I might have been a little ... mean to, um, Clive." I knew Clive wanted me to hang out with him at the dance even though he was playing in the band. He'd been trying to work up the courage to ask me. "I've been ducking him."

Silence hung in the room. "I think your friend may be in danger," Lucinda said gently.

Alice left the kitchen and came back shortly holding her huge book of fairy tales. "I'm sure some answers will be here."

But we didn't have time to wait. Jasper and I said goodbye and raced off to find Lea. In minutes we stood in front of the fence of Lea's house as night slipped down from the horizon. I'd hoped Lea would be hanging out near her fence like she sometimes did. In my mind we'd find her, warn her about her aunt; and fairy or not, I'd let her come and stay with me. No wonder she seemed so sad the last time I saw her. I drummed up my courage and began walking with Jasper up to that ramshackle house with the clattering shutters and menacing shadows. One look at the doorknocker made me hesitate for real this time.

The green brass dog's head stared viciously from above the door handle.

"Um," said Jasper. "This is probably a bad time to bring this up, but the Celtic mythology book said the banshee was often accompanied by a huge green dog that was her mascot."

I knew there was something menacing about that ugly thing.

Suddenly I imagined clanging that doorknocker, and the dog's mouth widening until I disappeared inside it forever – fairy magic could be so treacherous.

But I lifted the doorknocker anyway.

CHAPTER 20

Inside the Secret Garden

I BANGED FURIOUSLY, but no one was home.

What were we going to do?

Jasper and I had no choice but to go home and wait to try and contact Lea. All evening I kept checking out the window and turning on all the lights. I don't know why – maybe it was because of the eerie wailing that went on and on.

"It's certainly windy tonight," Mom commented. Except I knew that sound wasn't the wind, and that thought curdled my blood. Sookie gave me a start when I turned to go upstairs. She stood at the top of the stairs in her Valentine's nightie.

"Cindy phoned," she said, which is how Sookie sometimes referred to Lucinda because that's what Lucinda had called herself when they first met. Sookie excitedly dragged me to her hamster nest of a room, away from Mom.

Sookie whispered in a conspiratorial voice, "Cindy warned me about the banshee," as her eyes glowed with excitement. She never seemed to see past the adventure and understand the danger.

Buddy spun happily in his hamster wheel, oblivious to any peril. I figured you've sunk pretty low when a hamster's life looked better than your own.

"Cindy says that salt water is bad for banshees." Then Sookie began ticking her fingers off. "Silver is bad for banshees too. Rowan shoots are harmful to banshees. And some herbs ... rue and ... there was something else ..." Sookie scratched her head and looked upset she couldn't remember, but only for a second.

"I told Cindy I was very good with herbs. She seemed interested in that," Sookie said proudly. My sister loved being involved in grown-up stuff, as well as magical stuff.

It was my turn to rub my head as it began to ache with worry.

"I know about a secret herb," Sookie said slyly. "I watched when Bea wasn't looking, and she slipped the plant into her secret garden that day we all helped her."

"Oh yeah? What herb is that?" I asked, doubtful it would be any use to us.

"Wolfsbane. It's also called Cupid's Car. That's funny, isn't it? Because it's Valentine's."

Hilarious, I thought. Soul-sucking banshees were a riot.

"I don't have wolfsbane in my garden," Sookie said with a frown. "But Bea does. I wondered why she was keeping it secret, so during reading time at school I asked the librarian to help me find out loads about it." Sookie beamed proudly. "I've been doing a lot of my own computer research, just like you do, Cat. I know a lot more about plants now."

"Bea wouldn't grow something that was harmful to her," I pointed out. "Unless ... it was an important ingredient for something else," I said.

"Like a potion for making you look younger." Sookie smiled a secret smile.

I paid closer attention and started feeling sick. "Tell me what you know."

"At first I thought Aunt – I mean, Bea – kept the flower hidden because it's extremely poisonous, even if it touches skin. But now I'm thinking she keeps it because if she breathes the scent of the flowers under the moonlight, it can change her appearance.

"Huh?"

"Wolfsbane is a magical herb. When its tiny blue flowers bloom at night, the scent can make someone appear differently, even change into something else," Sookie explained patiently.

I remembered how I'd never seen Bea except after dark. Also, the ghastly image I'd seen at Lea's house had been in the window above the secret garden – as if she'd needed to breathe in the scent because the spell was fading.

"So those flowers could help someone ancient and evil look young and beautiful?" I gasped. The wolfsbane helped the banshee trick us about her appearance

Sookie, always one step ahead said, "Diabolical, huh Cat? But I know that if you pick wolfsbane while it blooms in the moonlight, the scent of the roots can harm a banshee. Or a werewolf or witch for that matter."

Okay, now Sookie was just getting silly – witches and werewolves only existed in books and movies. Seriously, we had enough trouble around here with evil fairies.

Except I now knew I had to sneak into the last place I ever wanted to go – Bea's garden – to cut some wolfsbane. I tried calling Jasper, but no one answered.

He wasn't online either. I tried contacting him a few more times.

I didn't want to go into that garden alone – if I could only reach Jasper.

I waited until Sookie fell asleep before I sneaked out of the house. Otherwise, she'd follow me and I couldn't do what I had to and watch her at the same time. It was getting really late when I threw small rocks at Jasper's window, but he didn't wake up. I knew this time if Mom caught me outside there would be no mercy. But I didn't have a choice.

I tried swallowing, but my throat felt dry as sandpaper. Tomorrow the dark moon would rise, so the waning moon was only a sliver of bone in a sky black as molasses. I told myself to stay calm, but as I slipped inside Bea's garden, I realized how unnatural it seemed. Thick brown vines twisted in the pot and reached their thorny fingers toward me when I came near, as if they were living creatures from a nightmare. I would have been badly scratched if I hadn't been wearing Sookie's gardening gloves for protection against the poisonous wolfsbane. She'd said even touching it would burn my skin.

Tree branches tapped a spooky death march on top of the garden shed while the wind shrieked through the branches and cut through my jacket in icy stabs. Winding Lea's scarf tighter around my neck, I crept to the tall hedge that surrounded Bea's secret garden and circled trying to find a way in. Finally I found a small space at the bottom of the hedge where there was a gap in the fence and I could slip my head through. Where my head went, maybe the rest of me would fit.

I had to find a way to stop the banshee. Clive's life might depend on it. Shoving into the leaves and branches, my head popped through below the gate, and my heart caught in my throat. Inside Bea's secret garden were strange and mystical flowers that glowed in sickly phosphorescence under the night sky. Some plants looked like giant toadstools and I thought of Ms. Dreeble's lectures on the animal kingdom and decided these were parasitic – they'd cause terrible harm to other plants. Some flowers seemed like little green Frankensteins, with creepy plant arms reaching straight up in the dark.

I wanted to crawl right back out, but instead I forced myself to scan the garden until I spotted the tiny blue flowers of the wolfsbane. Their overpowering perfume made me dizzy. I tried shoving myself further between the hedge and the gate, but I got stuck half way.

The door of Lea's house banged open, and I could hear the thump of footsteps on the porch. I stopped squirming and froze.

"What's out there?" commanded a chilling voice. "There better not be a cat in my garden!"

Sickened, my stomach twisted, and I was about to sink in fear when a voice whispered inside me. "She means a feline, not you." Then I forced myself to exhale carefully and turn and push until I burst through the hedge and under the gate, where I was swallowed up inside the belly of the secret garden. My lungs ached and I realized I hadn't even been breathing.

I gasped into my fist and lay still under the moonlight, but my heart pounded so loudly I was sure she could hear it.

"Here kitty," came the menacing voice. "Come try this special catnip I made for you." The voice came closer. I shuffled around and peeked through the hole in the hedge. Lea's aunt was dressed in a grey nightgown, and her long hair swept over her head as if she'd put her hand on a friction ball.

Her eyes glowed red!

I had to get away because I suddenly knew even if I wasn't the kitty she was looking for, it would still be the end of me. I didn't want curiosity to kill this Cat. Frantically, I searched the hedge for any opening, and then I found a darker space between the thorns and a gap between the fence posts. The only problem was that space led right into the graveyard.

The gate to the garden clicked as Bea fiddled with the lock. Running, I grabbed a handful of wolfsbane with my gloved hand and tugged until it came out by the roots. A latch lifted. I kept running. As the gate creaked open, I dived toward the space in the hedge and crawled out headfirst into the graveyard, the dirt sticking to my chin and filling up my nose. My scarf caught on a branch.

I squirmed, but I was trapped.

The hedge shuddered and leaves twitched as Bea kept searching for the cat. Surely she'd find me. A branch cracked just by my ear, and then I suddenly knew why I was so afraid of graveyards.

A small white hand reached from behind a gravestone and began tugging around my neck. I swallowed a scream, realizing a ghost had really come to take me away. Then my scarf became untangled, and I scrambled out from the hedge.

A blond head bobbed behind the gravestone, and I whispered in a wavering voice, "Sookie?"

"Quick," whispered Sookie as she stepped around the gravestone. "Hand me the wolfsbane." With Mom's garden shears, she snipped a piece of root and began to mash it with her mortar and pestle. A sickly sweet smell arose that almost made me choke.

"What is that stench?" shrieked Lea's aunt. "You horrible cat, I'll get you!" Even though I knew she was speaking about the furry kind of cat, I shivered as if she meant me. Then as Bea became seized by a fit of sneezing, Sookie feverishly mashed away at the root until we could hear Bea leave the garden and slam the back door.

"Let's get out of here," my voice shook.

"Good thing cats have nine lives," said Sookie, shaking her head.

I sure hoped so.

CHAPTER 21

The Heart's Deadly Beat

GROGGY AND HEADACHY, I sat at my desk in school the next morning as a slow tension built like a boiling witch's cauldron that threatened to spill over. It wasn't just me. During classes we snapped at each other as the girls led the boys around like puppies on a leash, and I couldn't focus my mind on anything except the dance and trying to stop the banshee.

Even though my friends didn't know about the banshee, at lunchtime worry creased their faces and haunted their eyes. Mia's eyelids drooped in exhaustion. "Why did I ever think having the boy of my dreams completely devoted to me would be fun?" She handed Mitch a sandwich and told him to bite and chew.

"This was so wrong," Amarjeet's voice clouded with regret, "to control someone like this." She steered Rabinder away from the stairs before he tumbled down. "Are you sure we should bring these guys to the dance, Cat? Shouldn't we get them to a doctor?"

"I'm sure. The charm can be dissolved under a dark moon." At least that's what Lea had told me. Lea hadn't shown up at school. I hoped she was okay. I couldn't forget the fear in her eyes that night in Sookie's room.

"Make sure the guys are there," I repeated. I wanted to keep all the guys together inside the gym in case the banshee went out hunting on Valentine's night. There were too many coincidences between Lucinda's dance and ours, and we'd be safer in numbers."

Then I searched for Jasper in the library. "I've got all the ingredients for stopping the banshee," I updated him. "Where were you last night anyway?"

Jasper closed the book he'd been reading, looked up, and said, "I wonder what will happen to Lea after we stop her aunt?"

"She'll be safe," I said. "That's the main thing."

Jasper and I agreed to meet early at the dance just in case there was any sign of trouble.

***

After dinner that night, I stood in front of my bedroom mirror. Mom had pinned my hair in an up-do. I stared at my new dress. It was everything I hoped it would be. The hot pink color made my dark hair shine and it toned down the green. The spaghetti straps and tulip skirt made me look older and more sophisticated. Lea's scarf draped around my shoulders and hung down the back, and I couldn't help think this was the coolest outfit I'd ever seen.

But none of it mattered anymore. And it was stupid to even wear a dress to the dance – I was setting out to stop a banshee – but Mom could never know this. The way magic worked around here, she'd never believe it or understand it. So I had to play along that this dance was going to be fun.

"You look beautiful," Mom said as she came into my

room and hugged me. "You worked hard for this dress. Oh Cat, I'm sorry you can't have a lot of wonderful things to wear like your new friend."

"I don't mind, Mom, really." And I totally meant it – there was nothing like constant danger to make you realize how nice clothes were low on life's priority list. Mom didn't even mention the outfit she'd been making for me.

"Wow," Sookie said as she waltzed in looking at my dress. "When can I be big enough to wear *that* dress?"

"Not for a long time, missy," said Mom, and she hugged Sookie too. "Stop trying to grow up so fast."

Mom didn't know the half of it.

I was grateful Sookie would be safe at home while Jasper and I tried to stop the banshee. I put on my coat and grabbed my heavy backpack.

Saying goodbye to my family, I swallowed my heart and left for the dance. The sky darkened as Jasper and I walked to the high school.

"The moon should rise soon," I said hopefully. "And all this will be over. We just have to be there for Clive." I stopped and reached in my backpack pulling out a plastic baggie. "I've got rowan shoots and wolfsbane."

Jasper nodded. He seemed to be in another world. This was strange as he usually was full of advice. When we approached the school and he still hadn't said anything, I asked, "Is something wrong?"

"I can't help but worry about Lea," Jasper said as he clutched the poetry book she'd given him. "What kind of life has she had living with an evil aunt?"

When my dad left and we had to move, I'd thought

there couldn't be anything worse. But Lea had it really bad, and I didn't know what would happen to her after we used the herbs to stop her aunt.

"I guess we just have to be there for her," I offered as we entered the school and headed for the gym.

Jasper nodded.

Darkmont's drab grey gym had been transformed into an enchanting palace. Old-fashioned Valentine foil hearts covered the walls and crepe streamers twisted into lace chandeliers. The Japanese lanterns glowed and swung in streams of pink and red light. As I stared up at the decorations all lit up, I couldn't shrug off the eerie sensation I'd walked into another time. After I took off my coat and smoothed out the wrinkles in my dress, a surprised voice called from the stage.

"Wow, Cat. You look a lot nicer than you usually do." The mixed compliment – of course – came from Clive, who had already set up for the band. *You have to save him even if he is a jerk*, I reminded myself.

Skeeter waited at the front of the stage with his drum and drumstick. I'd never seen him be so still. Briefly, I wondered why Sookie hadn't complained about how he got to be here and she didn't. As I looked around, kids began streaming into the gym. All the girls in the soccer team couldn't wait to get rid of their zombie dance partners.

Mr. Morrows and Ms. Dreeble arrived together as the dance chaperones. "You may want to unbutton your jacket, Deb," advised Mr. Morrows.

I don't know why, but it surprised me that Ms. Dreeble had a first name. Her fingers clumsily reached for the buttons and when she finally managed to take her coat off, I noticed a pajama sleeve fall down below her dress cuff. Her slip hung just below her dress and beneath that was a rolled-up pajama leg. My mouth fell open as I stared.

"I think ... Ms. Dreeble is feeling rather unwell," Mr. Morrows explained. *Stupid zombie ingredients*, I thought for about the hundredth time. Ms. Dreeble was the smartest person I'd ever met, and now she dressed herself as if she was a three-year-old.

Clive strummed his guitar and the two other guitarists matched his notes. The music began. Everyone began to shuffle around on the dance floor in the most pathetic dance I'd ever seen. Disgust flashed across Clive's face, and I heard him mutter again how this was a waste of his talent.

Then Skeeter began to play his drum. *Bong, bong, baruuum* – each bang seemed to echo my own heart's beat and fill me with rhythm as if I was hollow and had never understood music before. As Skeeter set the pace, the dancers began swaying and then fell into step under the glowing lights of the lanterns. And then they danced faster. And faster!

The boys and Ms. Dreeble snapped out of their zombie shuffle and began spinning their dance partners across the gleaming wood floor. My own arms longed to grab a partner, and my legs twitched to dance to the beat. Every single kid at the dance was being pulled onto the floor by a boy wearing the love charm. Soon everyone was spinning and jumping as the dancing built to a frenzied pace. Zach danced between five girls and threw Amanda in the air as he quickly turned to spin the next partner.

Then he'd turn back and catch Amanda before she landed – most of the time. Ms. Dreeble caught Mr. Morrows in a firm embrace and dipped him low to the floor as they began a tango.

Boom – boom, Skeeter banged his drum and the other band members kept the rhythm with their guitars. Clive's mouth opened in surprise, but he kept strumming madly. It seemed he couldn't resist if he wanted. Mitch and Rabinder tried to pull me onto the floor, but I dodged them and ran onto the stage and hid behind the curtain.

An alarm bell began clanging in my brain. I'd seen fairy dancing once before – and just like now, it wasn't pretty.

The gym door suddenly burst open to the outside, and people from the town filed inside as their legs dragged in a slide-step formation. Mr. Keating had Esmeralda firmly in tow as he launched the two of them onto the dance floor. Mia's mom dragged in Mia's father as they began tangoing like Mr. Morrows and Ms. Dreeble. Was that our vice-principal, Ms. Severn? She was dancing on the floor, spinning a surprised man into an amazing pirouette. Soon the gym was packed with people and the smell of Sookie's love charms of licorice, lavender, and dead stuff from the graveyard dirt. The smell became cloying and made my own head spin.

Wear the scarf, Cat, promise me, Lea had said. I tied the pink scarf over my mouth and nose and could immediately breathe easier. My head cleared just in time for a horrible thought. I watched the people on the dance floor dance with more speed and strength than the human heart could bear. Lea had said the charms would wear off

161

when the dark moon rose.

Would anyone last that long though?

Sweat poured from Ms. Dreeble and Mr. Morrows as they rocked in a deadly rhythm. Already kids were collapsing, only to jump back up, their faces white with exhaustion as they kicked higher and danced faster than any human could. Skeeter's face turned scarlet from his effort of pounding the drum. I looked around Skeeter's neck and he also wore a charm. Trust him to buy one from Sookie so he wouldn't be left out.

The gym door opened again, although this time with an almost supernatural hush. A grey figure crept in, and while I was sure it was Bea, her head was completely covered in a black veil. She let out an unearthly howl that sent me shivering until I pulled Lea's scarf one more time around my head and covered my ears. As the banshee screeched, the dancers pulled away from each other until they'd cleared a spot in the middle of the gym. Bea moved slowly to that spot – her long grey cloak dragging on the ground as if she was floating.

The dancers spun around her as they continued their frenzy. I rubbed my eyes as I saw a white glow flow from Bea's outstretched arms.

"Jasper, it's time!" I shouted.

But Jasper had disappeared.

CHAPTER 22

Dance of the Dead

BLOOD LEAKED FROM Clive's fingers as he frantically strummed his guitar strings. His eyes widened with horror as the dancing madness spun out of control. "Oh crap."

Clive took the words out of my mouth. What was I going to do? I'd searched in desperation for Jasper, but he wasn't here. The banshee stood in the center of the gym cackling wildly as she sucked the life from the dancers, and the dark moon rose in the night sky. All I had to stop Bea was wolfsbane and rue, and I wasn't even sure how I was supposed to use it – walk up to Bea and throw the stuff in her face?

Her horrible screeching broke into cruel laughter, and I realized I had to act fast. I grabbed my backpack, pulled out the baggie, and dumped its contents of wolfsbane and rue into my hand – and then yelped and dropped the herbs. I forgot wolfsbane was poisonous, and the flowers and roots burned my palm. Then I grabbed the baggie and wore it like a glove as I scooped the crushed plants from the gym floor.

Moving toward the shrieking banshee took forever as I pushed through the dancing dervishes. Bea saw me coming, but she only cackled.

"I see a cat *was* in my garden." Her hand moved to

lift the black net that hid her face. "Would you like to see under my veil? Will curiosity kill you, Cat?"

Dread spiked my heart. I got ready to throw the herbs just as Bea lifted her veil off her face. Then I froze.

Her face morphed into the image of a girl around my age, and in that fleeting second I knew it was the girl I'd seen in the newspaper article that had wrapped the foil hearts. It was Lucinda's friend Ann, the girl who had lured Gordie away and killed him. Then the face morphed into the one I'd come to know as Lea's aunt, and then, as if a wax mask sat on the stove, it melted into a pool of horror. Worse, her eyes were slashes of red light that glowed like a menacing jack-o'-lantern.

I couldn't force my own eyes off her – and I couldn't move.

Bea cackled, and its harsh cruel tone rattled against my eardrums as I stood unable to move. "It will take more than a few plants to stop me," she shrieked.

"Fortunately, we have more than a few herbs," a familiar voice said quietly. Alice and Sookie rushed toward me carrying the mortar and pestle that held smoking wolfsbane.

Of course there was no way my little sister would miss this calamity.

Sookie came beside me and stood on her tiptoes as she whispered, "Sorry, Cat. I forgot that burning the wolfsbane is what stops the banshee." A waft of the sharp, pungent smoke drifted toward Bea and she screamed before sinking to her knees.

Alice began circling behind the banshee and used a plant mister to spray salt water on Bea.

Sookie waved the smoke from the incense toward her, asking, "Should I use a bit more wolfsbane?"

The banshee's face melted into the young girl's image of Ann again before Bea shoved the veil back over her face and screeched.

But everyone still danced in a tortured fury.

Alice said, "This is only slowing her down."

Iciness flooded through my veins. The dancers would keep dancing until they died and Bea could then claim their souls for her own and regain her youth. I only had until the dark moon rose – after that, it would be too late. I wanted to slump to the ground until I woke up from this nightmare. Then a small voice inside me said, "You can't give up, Cat – you can't."

"More wolfsbane!" I shouted and threw my crushed blue flowers into Sookie's smoking mortar bowl. We waved the thick smoke right under Bea's nose. The banshee wailed and shrieked, making our skin crawl, and I had to fight the overwhelming urge to run and hide.

The dancers' faces were carved in agony. Mr. Keating was gasping for breath and clutching his heart all the while spinning Esmeralda as if she was an Olympic figure skater. Mr. Morrows's knees crumpled, but Ms. Dreeble dragged him along, sweeping the dance floor with her exhausted dance partner. Zach linked arms with two girls who had linked arms with three other girls, creating a deadly chain that whipped around the gym. Mitch kept tossing a frantic Mia up in the air and catching her like she was a football.

"Stop us, please," Amarjeet gasped as she and

Rabinder jumped up and down in a punishing pace.

Several dancing couples slumped to the floor, and I watched in horror as they pulled themselves up again like marionettes on strings and stumbled into a tortured and tangled dance. I threw whole buds of wolfsbane at Bea and she hissed like a cornered leopard. Then Bea let out an eerie, ear-shattering wail, but all the dancers kept dancing.

How could I have ever thought that creature was cool? I'd even wished my own mother was more like her. Then it hit me, a moment that seemed so long ago when we'd all been having fun hanging out together and digging Bea's garden.

"I have a special job for you," Bea had said, and she handed Skeeter a drum.

I ran for the stage. As if the drum sensed my intentions, the beat reached inside me and thrummed through my blood. *Don't think*, my brain commanded. *Just dance* – and I began swaying to the beat.

Promise you'll wear my scarf, Lea's voice whispered again, and I wound the length of scarf thickly around my ears. The scarf muffled the pounding in my head, and I ploughed across the stage like I was wading through mud. When I reached Skeeter, I grabbed his drum and pulled against it with my weight until I yanked it out of his hands. His drum beat was spurring on the dancers – the drum Bea had given him was part of the spell. I threw it to the floor and used both feet to stomp on the drum, puncturing the skin and breaking it to pieces.

Everyone in the gym collapsed, including the

musicians. Silence gushed like a soothing salve until the gym door burst open in a gust of wind, and Sookie uttered a small cry. I saw the tail end of a black veil fly out of the gym as if the wind had scooped it up and tossed it outside. I jumped off the stage and joined my sister and Alice on the dance floor.

"Bea has escaped." Alice's voice sounded exhausted, and she looked so frail I wondered how the wind hadn't knocked her down.

At first I didn't understand why there was a slow desperation rising inside me, except that I knew Bea would be a hungry creature on the hunt. That should have been frightening enough ... except there was a tiny thought trying to work its way through my panicked mind.

Then Sookie said in a puzzled voice, "Where is Jasper?"

Jasper was somewhere out there – possibly right in Bea's path.

"I think he might have gone to save Lea," I said in a worried voice.

"Lea?" asked Alice. "Who is that?"

"Bea's niece – we were worried what would happen to her if we tried stopping her aunt."

A tremor crept into Alice's voice when she said, "When Lucinda and I did our banshee research we discovered Beann shee has a sister. Her name is Leanne shee – the dreaded sweetheart fairy. She always wears green, and Cat ...

But I'd stopped listening because I now realized that Jasper had held that part back, the part about Lea and her name. Why? Did he not believe Lea could be evil either? Or was he trying to spare me? But I heard the last part of Alice's words.

"She lures poetic young men to their deaths."

CHAPTER 23

A Deadly Sweetheart

MY STOMACH LURCHED and for a minute I was sure I would be sick. My friend couldn't be that wicked, even if she was a fairy. I didn't believe Lea would harm anyone, but could she stop herself if her aunt forced her to do a terrible thing? I shook my head in confusion. "No – Lea's kind. I think she tried to help me against her aunt," I said stubbornly

"A dog can be a gentle companion, but it can also be a cold-blooded killer to rabbits," said Alice. "Lea's a fairy; she isn't human. And like an animal, she must obey her nature."

"Everyone has a choice," I said. "Even a dog ..." Doesn't it?

"Don't you see?" urged Alice. Under the glow of the lanterns she looked almost ghostly. "This is how Lucinda lost Gordie. He was a dreamer and a poet, and Ann lured him to his doom when she swept in after Lucinda had turned Gordie down. Now the grown-up Bea has tricked us. She was probably using this deadly dance not only to feed herself, but to divert us while Lea leads a boy to his doom."

I was about to say this was different, that Lea hadn't taken Clive away from me, but the words died on my lips.

All along I had thought there was a connection

169

between the two dances, and that a boy might die like Gordie did seventy years ago. I thought the spurned boy who was in danger was Clive, but Mia had also rejected a boy – the most poetic boy I knew.

"Oh no," I cried becoming convinced that my friend might not only cross paths with the deadly banshee, but that he was falling directly into her trap. He must have suspected that Lea was a sweetheart fairy, but he went off to find her anyway. Why would he do that? *Because she understood his pain*, a small voice whispered inside my head … *when you paid no attention*.

"We've got to find Jasper." I couldn't stop shaking as we headed for Alice's car, even when Sookie and I slid into the backseat.

"Where do you think Jasper and Lea are?" Alice sounded almost frantic as a cold urgency shrouded us.

"There's one place a fairy would be," Sookie said quietly, her face crumpled with worry.

No one had to say Grim Hill. We just knew.

Alice stayed close to the speed limit, but our town was small and in no time we pulled up behind the cemetery next to Lea's place at the foot of the hill.

"I want to come," said Sookie while I climbed out of the car.

"But I'll need your help if Jasper or Lea return to the house," said Alice. Sookie folded her arms across her chest and scowled, but she stayed with Alice.

I crossed through the graveyard, picking my way through the gravestones and crumbling statues, and even when I felt a tug on my dress and the sound of a tear, I didn't jump or shriek. I simply stopped and pulled my dress out of a tangle of brambles. I wasn't frightened of this place anymore. There were far worse things to fear than ghosts. When I made it to the trees, I remembered what Alice had said in the car.

"The sweetheart fairy is a lonely creature who is burdened with a terrible sadness."

I was forced to admit that sounded like Lea. Despite what Alice had told me, I truly believed Lea was sad because she didn't want to be wicked – and because she cared about our friendship. I heard a rustling and crept closer, hunkering down behind a bush and spying through a small gap in the leaves. I saw Jasper's back and Lea facing him with her arm outstretched. I dived through the bushes and jumped into the clearing.

"Jasper, come back to the dance with me," I said, trying to sound calm and not alarm either of them, even though my heart now pounded in my throat.

Jasper reached for Lea's hand, but he hesitated as I placed my hand on his shoulder. Then he shook me off.

"Lea needs me."

Lea said nothing but held her arm out to take Jasper's hand. Her eyes were bloodshot from crying.

"Let Jasper go," I begged her.

Lea said nothing as tears streamed down her face. Jasper stepped toward her and their fingers brushed. "Sorry, Cat," his voice strained.

"Please, Lea," I begged.

Lea kept weeping as she tried moving her mouth, and that's when I knew she was being forced to obey her aunt. Lea wanted to be good – and to prove me right, Lea lifted her arm as if she was lifting a heavy anchor. With great effort, she pointed to a book that bulged in Jasper's back pocket.

Speaking to Jasper, I said, "Lea's given you a way out." My thoughts raced. "She's a fairy and she's given us both fairy objects to resist the banshee's spell."

I unwound my scarf and dangled it in front of Jasper's eyes. "Jasper, Lea has given you a gift, a greater gift than you know. But you have to choose to use it."

As if in a dream, Jasper slowly reached into his back pocket and pulled out the poetry book Lea had given him.

"See?" I said. "Lea gave you poetry, and me a scarf. In her own way, she is trying to help us."

Lea chocked back a muffled sob and nodded.

"Fairy objects help us resist their glamour and break free of fairy spells. Lea's been trying to save us from her aunt and ..." my voice caught, "and ... trying to save us from herself."

Jasper clutched the book to his chest, and as if an invisible rope had been cut, he managed to stumble back from Lea.

Lea dropped her arm and lifted her green cloak to reveal the soccer shirt I'd given her. Then she shook herself and coughed before saying in a breathless, whispery voice, "You have been such a good friend, Cat, but now that I'm free, I have to leave." Then her voice lowered with despair, "I'm sorry to have caused you all this trouble, though I promise you, I will cause no one harm. Except there is one thing I cannot do – and that is stop my aunt."

Then Lea turned and began walking away. "But the dark moon is almost set in the night sky. If you can defeat the banshee soon, she will be forced to slink into some filthy hole and burrow her way back to Fairy, and she will not be able to return."

Defeat the banshee? All I wanted to do was run as fast as I could with Jasper and get back to the gym. Maybe we could get reinforcements.

Before Lea disappeared into the trees, she turned one more time and mouthed the word, "friend." Hanging my head, I almost turned away myself, except a flash of silver on the ground that shone in the dim shadows of the dark moon caught my eye. I spotted a mirror where Lea had been standing, and somehow I didn't think Lea had dropped that mirror by accident. I walked over and picked it up noting how the mirror was silver and carved with peculiar-looking plants and strange creatures. As I tucked the mirror into the belt of my dress, the hair on the back of my neck rose just before an eerie wail cut through the trees.

"Jasper, I think we'd better ..."

I turned to see the legs and feet of my friend being dragged behind the bushes and into a dark copse of trees as his poetry book lay in the dirt. I began running.

I ripped through the bushes as branches jabbed my legs and arms and shredded more of my dress. Between the trees, the banshee had wrapped her arms around Jasper and pulled him against her in a crushing grasp as another horrible, hungry wail escaped her ancient melting face.

My heart raced as I remembered Jasper saying, "Do you think someone is going to die?"

I knew the red glow of the banshee's eyes radiated a power that could freeze my heart and stop me in my tracks, so I averted my face as I ran up and tugged Jasper away. She shrieked; one of her arms shot out, and her clawed hand dug into my wrist. Something hideous tugged inside me as my soul was wrenched from my body, and I wondered if the person who was going to die might now be me.

Jasper scrambled to my side. He'd managed to break from her deathly embrace, and I heard him gasping for air as he tried to pull me. My whole arm ached from the cold as if I'd plunged it into a tub of ice, but I couldn't break away.

"C'mon, Cat." Jasper threw his weight back and tugged me harder, but the banshee spit and hissed and quickly clamped her other claw around my throat.

Iciness crept up my neck and into my jaw, and my teeth clacked together like a wind-up chattering skull. Soon my brain would freeze, and I wouldn't be able to even think.

"Don't give in."

I wasn't sure if that was Jasper or my own mind trying to rally me. But now my eyes ached from the cold and I wanted to just shut down ... when I suddenly wondered ... was there a way to freeze her like she'd first stopped me back in the gym?

An agonizing ache ratcheted up my arm, but I gritted my teeth and kept moving until I pulled the mirror from my belt and shoved it in front of the banshee, reflecting her own nasty eyes back to her.

Blood-red light shot out from the mirror as a piercing scream shattered the night, and Bea released me from her gasp. I stumbled back as Bea stood frozen to the ground.

"Keep the mirror in front of her," Jasper gasped as he forced air back into his lungs. "I have an idea."

As the dark moon set in the sky, Jasper gathered leaves and dried branches and made two piles, one on each side of the banshee. Suddenly I realized Jasper was using the tools of the ancient Celts. During Imbolic, to protect themselves, the Celts would build two bonfires and pass between them to invoke good luck and to leave ill fortune behind. A banshee was about as bad as fortune could get, I thought.

"Since the winter solstice, I always keep matches on me," said Jasper. We had both learned back then that Celtic people battled fairies with light and fire.

"Throw some holly on the fire as well." We'd also learned that certain plants, like holly, had strong fairy protection.

"I'm way ahead of you," said Jasper. Finally I could smell the pungent, reassuring scent of wood smoke and burning leaves. Then Jasper grabbed my free hand. "Let's pass between the fires."

The flames greedily licked the leaves and branches as I pulled away the mirror and ran past the banshee where I felt the fire's welcome heat on my frozen skin. Once we'd passed between the two bonfires, we turned and watched in horror as the banshee shrieked and wailed while she slumped to the ground and began digging through the dirt at an amazing speed until she crawled into a hole in the ground. Once she disappeared, Jasper and I pushed and shoved dirt and moss and everything we could get our hands on into the hole.

Then with our feet, we kicked up the hot ashes from

the bonfire and spread them on top of the ground to seal the hole and purify it against any fairy magic if the banshee tried to escape back to our world.

When we returned to the car, Sookie jumped out and ran to me crying. "Cat, I waited so long, I was so worried; but when Alice saw the smoke we knew no fairy would build a fire and that you were okay." Then Sookie gave Jasper a huge hug. Jasper might not appreciate it, but Sookie adored him. Still, he flashed a weak smile as he climbed into Alice's Austin Mini. As we drove back to the school, my sister asked, "Is Lea all right?"

I nodded as I noticed she never asked about Bea. I thought Sookie sensed through her weird connection to Fairy that Bea was gone for good.

At the school, the dancers were getting up off the floor, and the musicians stood on the stage looking dazed. Alice left, anxious to check back with Lucinda, but she suggested we try and make things seem as normal as possible.

"You might want to put on your jacket, dear," said Alice before she made her way back to the car.

Why? I had been freezing before, but we were now back inside where it was positively steamy from all the dancing that had gone on earlier. We climbed up on the stage, and Jasper asked one guitarist to switch to a slow waltz. Finally, there was some use for those stupid dance lessons.

"Last dance of the evening," Jasper announced into the microphone.

"I don't care; I want to sit down," complained Amarjeet. "I feel like my feet are going to fall off." She and

Rabinder stumbled toward the refreshment table and began downing soda.

Before the song finished, all the partners broke up, looking puzzled as to why they were with that person, let alone at a dance.

Ms. Dreeble noticed her pajama legs had slid down below her dress. With a small yelp, she ran into the girls' changing room.

Skeeter stood over his broken drum saying, "Really, Clive, I didn't step on it." When Skeeter spotted Sookie, he jumped off the stage and they ran and grabbed iced Valentine's cookies from a platter.

"You are a disgusting mess. Seriously." Clive grimaced.

It took me a minute to realize Clive was talking to me, and that it was as if I'd purposely annoyed him by not looking good. What was wrong with the way I ... But then other kids started calling out.

"What happened to you?" squeaked Mia.

"Are you okay? Did a car run over you or something?" asked Mitch.

"Looks like she rolled in compost," observed Zach.

I looked down and checked my nails. They *were* filthy – come to think of it, so were my hands. The pink scarf was smudged in muddy fingerprints. Then I noticed that one spaghetti strap had broken from my party dress, the tulip skirt hung in tatters, the bodice was caked with dirt and sweat, and my entire outfit had turned from hot pink to ash grey. The dress looked worse than the rags Mom kept in her dustbin. All that money ... all that work ... what a waste!

Meanwhile my two friends who had been so worried about their outfits looked great. Amarjeet had worn a red silk sari, and Mia had jazzed up a plainer dress with cool gloves, a belt, and gold chains.

When I ran my hand over my hair, all I could feel was the crunch of dried leaves.

"Don't worry, Cat. It's just that you're the ugliest anyone ever saw you," Skeeter said with blunt honesty.

Everyone fell silent and stared at me.

A leaf fluttered out of my hair and onto my dress. I flicked it off and stomped on it, crushing it with my foot. "Do I look like I care?"

And I didn't care – not one bit. Because something inside me had changed and I realized things would never be the same.

CHAPTER 24

A Grim Determination

MAGIC SLIPS INSIDE you when you're vulnerable and attacks your weakest spot. At least that's what I figured. Whenever I had a heart's desire to go to a nicer school, win a soccer match, or even to try to recapture the life I'd left behind in my old town, I let my guard down and disaster struck.

Not anymore.

It was as if a switch had clicked inside me and I was heading down a different path. Like on the soccer field, if I'd found out I'd never get the glory position of forward or goalie, then I'd have to play defense. From now on I was playing defense in this town.

It's not that I didn't care about the life I missed anymore, it was just that I figured out what was most important to me now.

Wicked fairies were not only locked up inside our fairy hill, it seemed magical creatures were drawn to it. At any time something bad could come our way. My family and friends needed someone to stand between them and the evil that roamed in our area.

That would be me.

Mostly nothing or no one else changed though. The day after we defeated the banshee, Sookie stomped her foot impatiently as she complained, "Cat, we'll be late, and Lucinda said she'd help me with my plants."

We met up with Jasper and headed for the Greystones'. Lucinda was waiting for us on her porch. She rocked in a chair, wrapped in a heavy blue quilt to protect her from the chill of a sunny February day. Even though she was getting better, I couldn't help but notice how her skin seemed paper thin as if she herself was slipping away. Worry gnawed me, but as we climbed the steps, she broke out in a smile and her eyes sparkled.

"I was out in my garden today," she said softly, "and I could feel Gordie's presence, sweet as a summer breeze blowing in from the west. I could hear the faintest whispers as if he'd come to say goodbye, and that he'd forgiven me."

"Like a ghost?" Sookie's eyes brimmed with curiosity. "A real ghost?"

Despite our latest disaster, my sister was still far too interested in the supernatural.

"Sookie, come show me your plant-growing skills." Slowly Lucinda got up from her rocking chair, took my sister's hand, and they headed for the back garden. Sookie puffed out her chest as she strutted past me.

Alice beckoned Jasper and me inside where we sat down on the red velvet sofa in her parlor, and I told her about my theory of magic and how it could trick a person and wreck their judgment.

"Magic traps me when I'm selfish," I finished and hung my head, ashamed at how I'd turned people in the town into zombies. "Look what we went through – all so I could have fun at a dance and keep the peace between my new friends and old friends. I keep thinking how if

Bea had won, what would have happened," I confessed.

"Cat's onto something," said Jasper. "I felt lonely and rejected and didn't care what happened around me. People could have been doomed, and I was busy writing love poems." He shook his head and I understood how awful that made him feel.

"I think you both are forgetting an important point," said Lucinda as she came through the kitchen. "You two have grave responsibilities, but ..."

"You are all only children," said Alice. "You're being forced to grow up fast and take on impossible tasks."

"Of course, you want to enjoy yourself and try to escape from the terrible burden of knowing what goes on inside Grim Hill," Lucinda told me, and then she turned to Jasper. "And you would like your affections returned."

"But we live in a magical place," warned Alice. "You can't forget that, but you also can't forget you are not adults. It's easy to get confused about what you want and what you must do. And because your sister is the youngest, she is the most vulnerable of all."

I gulped. "How does magic attack her?"

Alice's face brimmed with concern and she fiddled with a lace doily on her old-fashioned coffee table. "Magic doesn't attack Sookie. She's become a magical creature herself."

That was my worst fear. I grabbed a satin cushion and hugged it to my chest.

"But Sookie is good," Lucinda quickly reassured me. "That's why we have to guard her – because the powers of wicked creatures can work their way into Sookie still."

"How?" Jasper asked.

"Just as magic influences your desires, it works its way through Sookie's innocence," Alice said. "Sookie has no idea what a powerful magician she's become. It remains a game for her – a treacherous game."

"And you both can only do your best," Lucinda said, weariness creeping into her voice. She gazed at me, her grey eyes clear and grave.

"Remember, your feathers will always keep you from forgetting what happened here – unlike everyone else in this town."

We pulled our feathers from our belts, but I couldn't help wondering if they were much good to us anymore. They didn't stop Jasper from going after his heart's desire, or stop Sookie from practicing her magic at anyone's peril, and as for me ... well, I suspected something slightly different was going on with me.

Catching me drifting, Lucinda said more forcefully, "You don't have the luxury of forgotten secrets, so while you cannot afford to feel regretful or ashamed of your mistakes, you must keep the feathers to remember all the same."

Jasper and I promised Lucinda as Sookie came into the parlor and demanded Lucinda return to the garden with her. I quickly scolded my sister. "Sookie, leave your boots at the door."

"Stop bossing," Sookie folded her arms in defiance, but she stared at her muddy boots and her face turned red.

"Not to worry," said Alice. "I need to sweep up anyhow."

Neither of the Greystones seemed to mind she'd tracked dirt across their polished wood floor and onto their Oriental rug. But I minded that when they turned away, Sookie stuck her tongue out at me.

"We will help you for as long as we can," said Lucinda.

As I wondered what Lucinda had meant by that, I saw that she had to sit down in the chair and catch her breath.

***

Monday rolled around and on the way to school I wondered how my friends would greet me. But of course, no one seemed to remember much about the dance. Fortunately, fairy trances end up seeming like hazy dreams. The zombie incident was forgotten; but as if a shadow still hung in the air, I can't say there was a lot of chatter at our lockers in the morning. That is, until we saw a sign pasted on the gymnasium door: dance classes were over and soccer practice would begin again tomorrow after school.

Hope surged through me. Trading in my dance shoes for soccer cleats sounded great. "I can't wait to get back in the game."

"You can say that again," said Mia.

"And I want to clean the field with the guys," challenged Amarjeet.

"Oh yeah – as if," said Clive.

"Remember, we're supposed to pull together as a team, or who knows what else they'll have in store for us," I reminded them. The bell rang and I took off in a run along the dingy hallway.

"Cat, do you have your biology research paper?" Ms. Dreeble was back to wearing her hair in a ponytail, but she still wore her cool new glasses.

Oh no, not again. Finishing my report had vanished from my mind after battling and defeating banshees and saving people from a terrible fate. I hadn't thought of the report once during the weekend.

"Um, the research was taking a little longer than I …"

"I'm sorry, but you have used up all your excuses." Ms. Dreeble took out her mark book, and I didn't even want to think about what she was scribbling on the page. I figured it was only a matter of time before I was grounded – right after report cards to be exact. I sighed.

But I wanted to tell Ms. Dreeble how I understood "parasitic" and "symbiotic" perfectly now. That Bea had a parasitic relationship with humans and had wanted to drain them of their life so she could thrive. And that Lea and I truly did have a symbiotic relationship – how we'd helped each other and both of us had benefited. Except Ms. Dreeble wouldn't understand …

Mia leaned over and whispered in my ear, "That's just not fair. How can you get a bad mark when it wasn't even an actual assignment? No one else had to hand in a report."

The fact that my friend cared helped – a lot – even though once more, as things got back to normal, I seemed to always end up one more step behind.

Or did I?

When I walked home that day and passed the decrepit house where Lea and her aunt had lived, I realized something very important. I had sensed wickedness about that place right from the start – even when neither Jasper nor Sookie had felt a thing. I hadn't needed my feather to show me dark magic was at work. I'd felt that darkness on my skin, in the way chills prickled up and down my spine, and how my hair stood on end and tingled as if catching an electrical charge. What's more, I could even smell the pungent scent of dark magic in the air.

My own power was growing, but it wasn't magical like Sookie's powers. My power was more like a magic detector – a sort of fairy GPS.

Right this minute when I inhaled the chill air of the wind, I knew we were safe and we would be for a long while.

I wrapped my pink scarf one more time around my neck.

It was the cold that was making me shiver, right?

THE END

Uncover the secrets that started it all ...

The First Book from the "Grim Hill" Series

The Secret of Grim Hill

978-1-897073-53-7

Cat Peters is desperate to get out of Darkmont High. When she hears that Grimoire, the private school on the hill, is offering scholarships to the winners of a Halloween soccer match, she jumps at the chance. Her little sister Sookie and their neighbor Jasper try to tell her there's something *just not right* about the school, and their worries are confirmed when they uncover a mystery about a soccer team that disappeared years ago. Further investigation leads Cat to a book about ancient Celtic myth and fairy lore, and she soon realizes that there is something truly wicked at work inside the walls of Grimoire.

Winner, Ontario Library Association Silver Birch Award

Selected, Canadian Toy Testing Council's "Great Books for Children"

www.grimhill.com

The Uncle Duncle Chronicles:
Escape from Treasure Island
by Darren Krill / **978-1-897073-31-5**

Sage Smiley is going on vacation with his favorite uncle, world famous explorer Dunkirk Smiley (a.k.a. "Uncle Duncle"), using the powers of a magical talisman to go wherever he wants. But the aerial adventure goes awry when Sage's imagination brings them to Robert Louis Stevenson's *Treasure Island*. Together they must free a group of prisoners from the clutches of Long John Silver, lay claim to the glittering chests of pirate treasure, and fight for their very lives.

"... the next best thing to a sequel [to *Treasure Island*] ..."
– *Quill & Quire*

"Non-stop fun and action ..."
– *CM: Canadian Review of Materials*

"It's a rollicking adventure ... custom-made to spark the imagination ..." – *Edmonton Sun*

www.lobsterpress.com

About the Author:

Linda DeMeulemeester has worked in the fields of literacy and education for many years as a teacher and program adviser. She credits her grandmother, a natural storyteller who was born over a hundred years ago, for her love of mystery and suspense. Linda's short stories have been published in several magazines; *The Secret of Grim Hill* was her first novel.